THIS IS NOT A HOLIDAY ROMANCE

CAMILLA ISLEY

Boldwood

First published in Great Britain in 2024 by Boldwood Books Ltd.

Cover Design by Head Design Ltd.

Cover Illustration: Shutterstock

A CIP catalogue record for this book is available from the British Library.

Paperback ISBN 978-1-83633-352-4

Large Print ISBN 978-1-83633-353-1

Hardback ISBN 978-1-83633-351-7

Ebook ISBN 978-1-83633-354-8

Kindle ISBN 978-1-83633-355-5

Audio CD ISBN 978-1-83633-346-3

MP3 CD ISBN 978-1-83633-347-0

Digital audio download ISBN 978-1-83633-349-4

Boldwood Books Ltd
23 Bowerdean Street
London SW6 3TN
www.boldwoodbooks.com

1

NINA

I'm about to drop a bag of popcorn in the microwave ready for a rom-com marathon with my roommates when my phone pings with a message from my brother.

DYLANOSAUR

My dearest sister

Oof. With that opening, he's sure about to ask for something I'd rather clean my entire house with a toothbrush than agree to. Nuh-uh. I'm already wearing my pajamas ready for nineties Hugh Grant and bed, nothing more.

NINA

Whatever you're about to ask, the answer's no

DYLANOSAUR

Please. I'm stuck with one hand down the garbage disposal and I need you to come rescue me

I try to picture all the scenarios of how Dylan might've gotten into that predicament, but give up just as quickly. *I don't want to know.*

NINA

Can't your *angelic* roommate save you?

And by *angelic*, I mean spawn of Satan devil incarnate.

DYLANOSAUR

Tristan is away on a business trip

Pretty please?

I think longingly of the classic holiday movie we were about to watch and sigh.

NINA

On my way

DYLANOSAUR

I knew you were my favorite sister

NINA

I'm your only sister

P.S. Lucky you had your phone on you before you got stuck

DYLANOSAUR

Actually, I'm dictating. My phone is in the living room

NINA

Is your phone's virtual assistant reading my answers aloud to you?

DYLANOSAUR

Yes

> Alexa, please play Justin Bieber's latest album at top volume

I smirk, imagining my brother shouting a counter order to be heard over the music. With a sigh, I drop the still-closed bag of popcorn back into the box and prepare to tell my roommates movie night is over for me.

"How long is that popcorn taking?" Hunter asks, as if on cue.

I exit the kitchen and find her kneeling on the couch, her hands on the backrest, straining her neck to check what I'm doing. Her wavy dark hair frames her face as she balances at a weird angle.

"Roomies," I announce, stepping fully into the living room. "I'm sorry, but I'm going to have to call a raincheck on rom-com night."

"No, why?" Rowena asks. The light catches on her glasses as she looks up from her phone, her chestnut braid swaying with the movement.

"I have to go save my idiot brother from himself."

Hunter's eyes get a little brighter at the mention of Dylan. "What happened?" she probes, her curiosity thinly masked.

"He's trapped himself in the garbage disposal," I explain, putting away my phone and pulling on a puffer jacket.

"Can't the Prince of Darkness save him?"

I chuckle at Rowena's use of our favorite nickname for my brother's evil roommate. "On a business trip, the useless prick." I ready myself to brave the cold, pulling on my Uggs over my pajamas. "If I hurry, I can be back in time to watch the movie."

"You're going in your PJs?" Rowena questions, pushing her glasses up the bridge of her nose.

"Yep, it's only a couple of blocks. I'm not getting dressed again."

"We should go with you," Hunter suggests eagerly.

I frown. "Why would you want to go out in the freezing cold?"

"Your brother and the Prince of Darkness have a huge TV," Hunter explains, blushing slightly.

"And they have premium cable," Rowena interjects. "We could watch something new, instead of rewatching *Love Actually* for the millionth time. It's only a couple of blocks, as you said."

"Plus, you shouldn't walk around the city alone at night," Hunter insists.

"It's decided," Rowena declares "We're moving the pajama party to your brother's place."

Dylan will be grumpy about the home invasion, but he's the one who needs rescuing. I shrug. "Let's go."

* * *

I use my spare set of keys—the fact that I have them irks the Prince of Darkness to no end and is also why I'll never give them back—to let myself into my brother's building.

I know I'm in trouble when we step out of the elevator and hear the distant notes of a Justin Bieber song. The volume intensifies as we reach the corner unit—because my brother, the investment banker, and the Prince of Darkness, CEO of an evil tech corporation (I don't really understand what his fintech company does but it must be something wicked if he runs it) live in the most expensive apartment on the top floor. Which, with New York's real estate prices, would still have been impossible even with their fancy jobs. But Tristan's father, probably Satan himself, gifted the place to his little mini demon as a graduation present. Dylan pays him a lowball rent, and they split expenses.

As I unlock the door and step into the apartment, the decibel level of the song becomes unbearable. I dash into the wide-open space, all modern furniture and wall-wide windows, trying to locate a shutoff button. From his half-reclining position over the sink, my brother stares murder at me but still points with his free hand to the smart speaker assistant on the shiny crystal coffee table.

When I pulled the prank on Dylan, I hadn't expected him not to be able to shut off the album. But I didn't consider that the sound system in Satan's lair is concert-level loud. Dylan's bad for his poor taste in roommates.

To make the music stop, I have to physically grab the speaker, bring the AI out in the hall, and impart the instructions where she can hear me. When I come back, Dylan is being interrogated by Rowena on the dynamics of his accident while Hunter just stares at him, lost in some sort of trance.

"I dropped my ring," Dylan explains.

I roll my eyes as I remove my outer layers and pull my natural dark blonde hair up in a topknot. I hate that stupid ring. When my brother and the Prince of Darkness won the basketball national championship in their senior year at Duke, it was all anyone could talk about—*for months*. Over and over, I had to listen to how many blocks Dylan pulled off, how many shots from three Tristan sunk, and what a glorious game it was. One that I was forced to witness *in person*, to show my sisterly supportiveness. I wouldn't have minded if it were only Dylan playing. But having to stomach number 666 swagger through the entire two halves, making acrobatic dunks, and sending more than one cheerleader to the emergency room with fainting spells was just too much—666 definitely wasn't Tristan's number, but that's how I like to remember it.

I roll up the sleeves of my pajama top and step into the kitchen, beaming at my brother. "So, what do you want me to do?"

Dylan glares at me. "You left me in Bieber hell for half an hour. I'm going to strangle you the second I get free."

Keeping a safe distance, I hop onto the black marble counter—black souls must come with black fixtures. "I'm glad you brought that up in advance, dearest brother, so we can negotiate the terms of your release."

"Nina, I swear—"

"Hush, hush... here are my terms." I count off my fingers. "I get an immediate pardon for the Bieber incident—I'm sorry, by the way, I didn't know your speakers could produce a sonic boom."

Dylan stares daggers at me but nods.

"I'm going to need verbal confirmation."

"Apology accepted," he grits out. Not like he has a choice. "And what else?"

"Me and the girls get to watch a movie of our choosing on your superior appliances and cable service."

"Yeah, why did you bring the entire cheer squad?" He pushes his fringe of blond hair—unfairly lighter than mine—out of his face.

"We're here for protection," Hunter squeals a bit too loud. "Couldn't let your sister walk alone in the middle of the night."

"It's not the eighties," Dylan protests.

"They're here for the premium streaming, mostly. Do you accept our terms?"

My brother's eyes gleam with playful spite. "Next time one of your toilets clogs and you don't know what to do, I'm going to have so much fun telling you to call a plumber."

I cock my head. "Do you wish me to add unlimited plumbing support as a provision?"

"No. I take the deal."

"Perfect." I hop off the counter. "You gals pick a movie while I solve this."

"Do you have popcorn?" Hunter asks my brother.

"Second cabinet to the left."

She finds the snacks and pops them into the microwave—also black. "Thanks."

"How do I free you?" I ask Dylan.

"There's a toolbox under the sink in the laundry room. You're going to need to unscrew the disposal from underneath."

That's how, ten minutes later, I end up with a deluge of triturated, decomposing, wet refuse on my chest. "Ew." I emerge from under the sink. "You owe me big time for this brother, big time."

"The Bieber thing makes us even," Dylan says, massaging his wrist.

"I'm going to need a shower."

"Be quick," Hunter calls from where they're nestled on the gigantic sectional couch. "We want to watch the movie."

"Trust me, no one wants to be rid of this garbage faster than me."

I step out of the kitchen, wiping my dirty hands on my already ruined flannel PJ top, and freeze when I hear a key turn in the front door's lock.

I'm still frozen in place when the Prince of Darkness enters the apartment and finds me standing in his living room with sewage running down my chest and smelling like the aftermath of a skunk convention.

2

NINA

No matter that my hands are still half covered in slime, the moment I spot Tristan, I reach up and undo the topknot on my head, smoothing my hair down to cover my jug ears.

I know, I know. I'm supposed to love my body as it is, and jug ears are nothing to be ashamed of. I should own them as part of myself. And I mostly do, unless in the presence of the Prince of Darkness.

Our eyes lock across the room. I take in his expensive suit, wrinkled after a long flight, his elegant coat, trolley, and slightly less-than-perfect hair. The dark circles under his eyes that, unfortunately, don't make the blue of his irises any less piercing. He does the same and inspects my shoeless feet, flannel PJs, and the muck running down my front.

He raises an eyebrow, giving me a curt nod. "Gremlin."

One word. One word out of his fucking mouth and my hate for him flares.

Before you pick sides or call me exaggerated, I should probably give you a little context. The first time I met Tristan Montgomery was fifteen years ago, when we were thirteen and eighteen, respectively. It was around this time of year, December 20. He and Dylan had had a game in New York on the 19th, and instead of going back to Duke, they came straight to mine and Dylan's hometown, Mystic, Connecticut, to spend the holidays.

Tristan's family had ditched him for Christmas or something, I don't remember. But I know that at the time I felt sorry for him. Now I understand why not even his parents would want to spend winter break with him.

Anyway, the second my brother walked into the house with his tall, dark-haired, blue-eyed friend, I had a crush. An infatuation so all-consuming that I was ready to tear down all my Adam Levine posters from my bedroom and replace them with Tristan Montgomery ones. I would've traded all my *Twilight* books, even the limited editions, for a simple nod from him.

In all my years of sharing a house with a basketball player, I had never taken notice of Dylan's athletic build the same way all my friends seemed to. To me, his six-foot-five frame, muscular arms, and broad shoulders were completely normal. Unremarkable even. But on his best friend, I noticed. Oh, I noticed.

What can I say? I was young and naïve.

For the first few days, I was too shy to even say good morning to Tristan. Then one night, I gathered my courage and made an approach. He and my brother were playing video games in the basement after dinner, so I made hot chocolates for the three of us. I brought the mugs down and, after delivering them to the boys, I went back up the stairs, pretending to leave. Instead, I sat on a high carpeted step hidden from view. I pulled my knees up while I sipped my chocolate, waiting to eavesdrop if they'd say something about me.

Guess how well that went.

"Dude," Tristan snickered, "you didn't mention you were living with a gremlin."

"Don't be a jerk," Dylan chided him.

"I'm not being a jerk, she's cute." There was a muffled oof from Dylan, maybe Tristan elbowing him. "Come on," he continued, "don't tell me you've never noticed the resemblance. Big eyes, wild hair, floppy ears."

In my defense, I still hadn't discovered the use of hair conditioner and my hair was a frizzy mess that could've very well made me resemble a crazed gremlin. By some miracle, I also had sailed through all my previous eight grades of school without being bullied or made fun of because of my jug ears. I had never been too self-conscious about them until that night.

With my heart already broken by his mean comments but a glutton for punishment, I peeked through the railing to see what they were doing. Tristan was mewling while cupping both his ears, making them jut out.

I saw red. I lost all rational thinking and stormed down the stairs, screaming, "You're an asshole!" Not contented, I threw my hot chocolate at Tristan, hitting him in the center of his Blue Devils hoody. I ruined the sweatshirt but didn't cause any burns—regrettably.

The last thing I heard as I stomped away was Tristan asking my brother, "Man, did you feed her after midnight or something?"

It was rampaging hate between us from that night on. The next time I saw him was the following summer. My hair was subdued into a perfect shine and left unconstrained to cover my ears for the entire extent of his visit. Even if he kept throwing me in the pool as a declared retaliation for ruining his favorite hoodie. And the constant surprise splashes made the effort to keep my hair dry and glossy seem futile. He also still called me Gremlin and hasn't stopped ever since.

Our feud has only intensified over the years. On the too-frequent occasions I've been forced to stomach his presence, it's been an all-out war. We started with childish skirmishes, like my habit to tie his shoelaces together—unfortunately he fell flat on his nose only the first time. Or the way I'd constantly change his gaming profile name in our basement to varied insults. And that one time I put bleach in his shampoo—orange-haired Tristan was a sight to behold. That same night, he put a Bluetooth speaker in my room and convinced me I had a ghost in the closet, I've never been so scared in my entire life.

Over the years, we've evolved into more grown-up pranks. I've signed him up for multiple dating profiles stating he lived with three cats, wanted to get married as soon as possible, and have five kids. I gave away his real phone number, which he's had to change twice. With that face, the calls just kept on coming. I don't have proof, but for every spam call or email I receive for services I never signed up for, I know Tristan is behind it. The first year I moved to New York, he stole Dylan's phone and told me to come to my brother's birthday party in a costume. Let's just say the bunny scene from *Bridget Jones* has nothing on me. I tried to own my cheerleader getup with pride, but he kept smirking all night and it just ended with me throwing my pom-poms at him.

That's why now, as we linger into this sort of standoff, I study my next move.

He's just come back from a business trip. He looks tired, and definitely less polished than his usual perfect appearance. If it were me returning home after a long day of work and exhausting traveling, I'd want to wash away the grime and go to bed.

Coincidentally, a necessity that puts us in direct conflict because there's no way I'll wait until I get home to wash the filthy goo that's seeping through my pajamas.

Now, his swanky apartment has two bathrooms, of course. But only one has a shower. And while I'd love to soak in the tub. I also know that Tristan Montgomery doesn't take baths—imagine Satan soaking in bubbles, not happening. The primary bath is basically Dylan's personal bathroom. I don't think Tristan has ever stepped foot in it.

I stare at the door of the bathroom with the only shower in the house and give the Prince of Darkness a feral grin.

He follows my gaze to the door and back to me. "Gremlin, don't you dare."

But I have the advantage. I'm already halfway there.

Without a second of hesitation, I sprint down the hall, pumping my arms as I run. I hear him chasing after me. But despite his superior build and longer legs, I reach the bathroom door first and get in.

I've barely turned the lock when there's a dull thud on the other side as all 200 pounds of muscular asshole crash against it.

Then the pounding starts. "Gremlin, get out of that bathroom. I'm not kidding."

"I'm sorry. What was that?"

"I'm tired. I don't have time for your bullshit."

"What? I can't hear you. Guess we'll have to wait to catch up until after I take a very looooong shower."

I turn on the faucet to drown out his protests. As the water warms, I pluck my dirty clothes off, trying not to gag. But before I step under the jets, I shoot a quick text to my roommates' chat.

NINA

Start whatever cheesy rom-com you selected and don't let the Prince of Darkness bully you into shutting it down. We're owed a movie

WINNIE

Won't you miss the movie that way?

NINA

Knowing the Prince of Darkness will have to watch it will be my solace

WINNIE

> But it's the new enemies to lovers, fake-dating
> one we saw the trailer for the other night

Oh no, I really wanted to watch that movie. It was just in theaters and it's going to take ages before it becomes available on our lesser subscription. But this is war, sacrifices must be made.

NINA

> Let it roll, I'll watch it another time

HUNT

> We just pressed play

> I'm seriously worried TPOD will murder us now

NINA

> Don't worry, Dylan won't let him. My brother
> owes us

With that last mental image of Tristan ousted from his favorite bathroom and forced to watch quality romance footage, I welcome the embrace of the warm water for the longest fucking shower I'm ever going to take.

3

TRISTAN

When it's clear no amount of pounding will make my best friend's little sister come out of the bathroom, I give up.

After the crappy week I had, a showdown with Nina Thompson is the last thing I needed. Well, too late. She's won this round, but the game is far from over.

I walk back into the open space living room to find two other minxes sprawled on my sectional, eating my popcorn, and watching my TV. Dylan is perched at a safe distance on the other side of the couch.

I look at my roommate with a silent frown spelling, *What the fuck, man?*

He smiles apologetically. "I got stuck in the garbage disposal. They were the only ones who could help."

That revelation attracts my gaze to the kitchen, where random parts of the waste disposer are scattered on the tiles with a trail of yuck leaking from under the sink.

"Don't worry about it," Dylan says. "I'll clean it up tomorrow."

As if I could sleep knowing there's *that* on my kitchen floor.

I remove my suit jacket and roll up my sleeves. I'm already

kneeling with my head under the sink, screwing the first piece back on, when Dylan squats next to me. "I said I'd do it tomorrow."

"Pass me the wrench."

Dylan hands me the tool and sighs, proceeding to mop the floor while I finish reassembling the disposal.

By the time I'm done, the kitchen is once again clean, and Dylan is leaning on the mop, eyeing me with a goofy expression.

"You know, leaving it for one night wouldn't have killed you. You need to relax."

"No, I need a shower." Now more than ever. "What I *don't* need is to come home after a long day and find your sister in my bathroom, her roommates on my couch monopolizing the TV, and the kitchen a fucking mess."

Before Dylan can reply, I hightail it to the living room. I don't want to direct at him anger that mostly has to do with the crappy text I got from my mother just a few hours ago.

As I sit on the armrest of the couch, waiting, my mood doesn't improve. I keep checking my watch every other minute. Dylan sits next to me after a while, presumably after cleaning the sink base cabinet. My best friend becomes absorbed in the stupidest movie I've ever watched. Two people who supposedly hate each other pretend to date at a destination wedding for a bogus reason until they go at it like rabid rabbits.

This is torture.

When Nina still hasn't come out of the bathroom thirty minutes later, I burst out, "How long can a shower last?"

One of the roommates, the one with the wavy dark hair, turns to me. "Regular woman shower? Half an hour, easy." She tilts her head mockingly. "Revenge shower? I'd say an hour minimum."

"Revenge for what? I didn't do anything."

"You probably called her Gremlin at least once," the roommate with the braid explains.

"Not my fault if she can't take a joke."

"Joke's not funny if you're the only one laughing." The dark-haired one again.

Dylan makes a hand-over-throat gesture, signaling to cut it because I can't win, or because we're outnumbered. I'm not sure about the why, but the message is clear: I should not complain about his sister taking her sweet time in *my* shower.

Like hell.

After another twenty minutes, I've had enough. I storm back down the hall, and just as I'm about to pound on the door again, it opens.

Holding a ball of her dirty clothes under her arm, Nina blinks. She's wearing nothing but a white towel—*my* white towel. Her long wet hair frames her face, and her bare shoulders are dotted with tiny droplets of water that shine like crystals. I suddenly have to fight an instinct to run a finger over her collarbones and smear the water over her skin.

Our eyes meet, linger for a heartbeat, then she glances at my rolled-up sleeves before her gaze collides with mine again, more intense this time. "You've been standing here this entire time?"

"That is my towel," I clip.

In response, she bends her chin to sniff the hem. "Really? It doesn't smell like dead puppies. I hadn't figured."

My jaw ticks. "I want it back."

"I'll just go change in Dylan's room and I'll bring it back."

She makes to walk down the hall toward Dylan's room, but I shoot out an arm to block her.

Nina frowns. "What are you doing?"

No idea.

But she's rubbed me the wrong way tonight. "I want it now."

"Now?" Her voice comes out small.

My hand flat on the wall, I smirk. I have her. After years of spoken and unspoken challenges neither of us has ever backed down from, I finally have her. "You've got a problem with that, Gremlin?"

Her jaw sets. I'm not sure if it is for my use of her nickname—I didn't know it still bothered her so much after fifteen years—or if it's about the dare. We do a lot of those. I can't remember a time I saw her when some kind of challenge wasn't involved.

As a rule, we try to avoid each other as much as possible, but when we find ourselves in a group situation because of Dylan, the knives come out.

There was that time we were at the Hamptons out of season, and she snickered that I was too much of a wuss to go into the ocean for a swim. I only just avoided going into hypothermia, but pretended I bathed in frigid waters all the time. Or when I told her she couldn't out-drink me, and we both ended up almost needing our stomachs pumped—Dylan wasn't happy; it was his birthday. That was a night to forget, admittedly. But another one of Dylan's birthdays—the one where I tricked Nina into coming dressed as a cheerleader—still is one of the funniest nights I've ever had. Probably one of the few where I had the upper hand. And even when I don't, I never give up, I never back down. And neither does she.

Once she dared me to ride the Cyclone at Coney Island three times in a row after we had a hot dog feast. I puked after ride two but still went for number three. One night, I picked all her karaoke songs, from Eminem's "Godzilla" to Celine Dion's "My Heart Will Go On." She rapped her way through every verse and broke our ears with each off-key high note, but she sang them all. I swallowed a ball of wasabi on one occasion not to give in. She ate a mega-stack of pancakes, complete with a mountain of whipped cream and syrup, to prove me wrong. It was like watching Khaleesi eat an entire horse's heart. No matter that she was forcing down fluffy pancakes and not raw meat. Nina once bet me I wouldn't go to a Knicks game wearing a Boston Celtics jersey. I almost got lynched.

The point is, retreating from a challenge isn't something either of us knows how to do. Our score is tight as of now, nil to nil. But tonight, I have her under my thumb. Because there's no way Nina Thompson will drop her towel in front of me.

We stare at each other for what feels like a minute of solid eye contact before she takes a step back.

"Very well."

She unhooks the towel from around her torso and, shuffling awkwardly with the clothes in her arms, she drops it to the floor—eyes never leaving mine.

I do my best not to watch, not to let my gaze drop by even a fraction of an inch. But my peripheral vision is more than enough, I can see *everything.*

I'm suddenly very aware that my best friend—also her six-foot-five, protective, muscular older brother—is just in the other room. *What am I doing?*

* * *

Nina

As I drop the towel, holding his stare, there's more than just murder churning in Tristan's eyes. What exactly is swirling into those evil depths, I cannot tell. And I'm not about to sit around naked to find out. My supply of boldness is about to run out.

With as much dignity as I can muster, I clear my throat and, gesturing to the arm still blocking my way, I ask, "Do you mind?"

Tristan drops his arm, and I proceed the short distance to my brother's room, resisting the urge to cover my butt with the ball of clothes in my hands as I go. I can practically feel Tristan's gaze metaphorically slapping my ass.

Then I'm in Dylan's room. Safe. Hidden behind a solid wooden door. Oh gosh, what was that? I'm not even sure who won this one. I only know my heart is hammering way too hard against my ribcage.

To distract myself, I drop my dirty PJs on the floor and rummage through Dylan's chest of drawers to find something clean to wear.

My brother's clothes are not just oversized for me, they swallow me whole, but at least they're freshly laundered and warm.

Which gives me an idea. I pick up my soiled pajamas and move to the laundry room, where I dump them in the washing machine and set the cycle to the most intensive, highest temperature one. I'm not concerned about ruining my flannels with aggressive washing. All I care about is that Tristan "I-Want-My-Towel-Now" Montgomery will lose water pressure and possibly even have to take his precious shower cold.

4

NINA

Two days after rescuing Dylan and having to interact with his evil roommate as a result—no good deed goes unpunished—I walk into my parents' cozy home in Connecticut. As I remove my coat in the hall, I'm greeted by the smell of Mom's pecan pie and the soft glow of holiday lights. The familiar creak of the floorboards underfoot makes me feel like I'm stepping back into my childhood. To a time when their squeak was my worst enemy on the nights I was trying to sneak in past my curfew.

"Welcome home, honey," Mom says, enveloping me in a warm hug.

"Hey, kiddo." Dad joins us, his eyes brimming with affection. "How was your trip?"

"Exhausting, but good," I reply, breaking free from Mom's grip.

Dad comes up behind me, resting his hands on my shoulders. "Just in time before the storm breaks. Looks like we're in for a big one."

"They're saying two feet of snow," Mom adds.

I glance out the window at the barren trees, their gnarled

branches reaching up into the gray sky. A light flurry has already begun to fall, dusting the ground in white.

"Go into the living room." Mom shoos us away. "I'm going to make hot chocolate for everyone."

While I remove my outer layers, my dad brings my suitcase up to my room, making his usual joke. "What did you pack in here? A dead body?"

We settle in around the fireplace, mugs of hot chocolate in hand, as the news drones on about flight cancellations and road closures.

"I hope Dylan will be okay driving up tomorrow," Mom worries, furrowing her brow. "It's a pity you two couldn't come together."

"Not my fault he's a workaholic. I wasn't about to waste a day because he wants to work on the Saturday before Christmas."

"Oh, you know how it is at his bank," Mom coos. "But it's great that with Christmas coming on a Wednesday, we'll have an entire week together. I love having you kids at home." She stares out the window with concern. "I just hope the weather doesn't get much worse before Dylan gets here."

"He'll be fine," Dad reassures her. "Dylan knows these roads like the back of his hand. Besides, that truck of his can handle anything."

Mom sighs but says nothing more, staring into the crackling fire.

As night falls, I drift off to the familiar sounds of home—the old house creaking, the wind whistling outside, and Mom and Dad's hushed voices as they watch TV downstairs.

The next morning, I wake to a winter wonderland. Snow piles up against the frost-kissed windows, sunlight glinting off the new icicles dangling from the roof while iridescent flakes swirl in the air.

Reports of JFK shutting down filter through the news as I pad into the kitchen, still clad in my fuzzy green pajama bottoms and coordinated Grinch slippers.

"Morning, sunshine!" Mom greets me. "How did you sleep?"

"Like a log," I admit, grinning as I snag a piece of buttered toast from the counter. "It's amazing how quiet it is here."

"Isn't it?" She smiles, pouring me a steaming cup of coffee. "No honking taxis or loud neighbors."

"Exactly what I needed." As I sink into a chair at the kitchen table, my gaze wanders to the opposite head of the table, where Dad is engrossed in the weather report. "So, JFK's closed, huh?"

"Seems that way," he replies, not tearing his eyes away from the screen. "A lot of people will be stranded for Christmas."

"Good thing Dylan is driving, then." I take a sip of my coffee. "Any word on when he's arriving?"

"He should get on the road soon," Mom chimes in, glancing at the clock. "Your father already checked, and the I-95 is still open, thank goodness. Dylan should arrive just after lunch."

Which means I can enjoy another morning of being exclusively pampered by my parents. After breakfast, I curl up on the sofa, losing myself in a book. In New York, I don't get much quiet time. I work for a climate tech company designing and testing carbon mitigation systems. Our mission is to speed up the shift toward net-negative emissions through our innovative CO_2 monitoring and mitigation technologies, alongside our platform that provides real-time, actionable data.

It's a rewarding job, but demanding. And living with my two best friends, I'm seldom alone. I'm not complaining. But it will be nice to have a morning of peace and quiet with nothing to do but read and eat the food someone else made for me.

By early afternoon, the storm is in full swing again. Strong winds shake the shutters and rattle the windows, snowdrifts reaching up to the gutters. Still lounging in my pajamas, I rummage through the pantry for a snack. I find a bag of Cheetos and, since Dad is watching a game in the living room and I want to keep reading my book without being distracted by his commentary, I retreat to my room.

Upstairs, I reach a new level of laid-back. I'm eating in bed—a paperback in my lap, a bag of chips on one side, a can of soda on the other—using my white T-shirt as a napkin before I turn the pages so as not to smear the novel with Cheetos powder.

I've just reached a juicy chapter when I hear the crunch of tires on the snowy driveway and soon afterward a car door slamming shut.

Dylan!

With a tingle of anticipation, I bound down the stairs, eager to greet my brother. But as I approach the front door, I spot a familiar silhouette through the frosted glass. Tall, broad-shouldered, with tousled black hair. Definitely *not* Dylan. My steps falter.

It can't be. Tristan was supposed to fly back to San Diego yesterday. I rub my eyes, convinced I'm seeing things, but when I look again, he's still there, presumably waiting for someone to let him in.

I'm not letting him in. In fact, I'm considering how fast I can board the door when Dylan's voice drifts in from the front yard.

"Get in, it's open."

The handle turns, and I freeze at the bottom of the stairs as the door slowly opens.

Familiar blue eyes stare back at me, at once puzzled and mocking.

It's really the Prince of Darkness. In my house, at Christmas. *Please, not again!*

I stare at him, stunned speechless. And this odd moment passes where I notice every detail of his face—the slight wrinkle of

Tristan's brow, his too-perfect eyebrows, that cruel, luscious mouth. My heart nearly leaps out of my chest as a thousand questions race through my mind and the uncomfortable silence stretches between us. What is he doing here? Why is he not in San Diego?

A cold draft of the winter storm blows into the house and the icy air hits me, providing an answer to my questions. The news about flights being canceled and JFK shut down jumps at the front of my mind, and the horrific reality dawns on me. Please tell me Dylan didn't invite the Prince of Darkness to spend the entire holidays with us because I'm going to have to commit a fratricide.

But before I can go murder my brother, my first instinct is self-preservation. I reach up and fumble with the hair tie, releasing the messy bun keeping my hair up and allowing my long blonde locks to cascade around my face. I smooth the strands down to cover my ears—no matter that my fingers are still Cheetos dirty—and fluff them a little over my front.

Tristan follows the gesture. Then his eyes flit downward to my chest for a split second, and a hint of discomfort flickers across his face.

I track his gaze to my white T-shirt, covered in orange finger-tips, and to where my nipples have gone rock hard—because of the cold air blowing in. No other reason. I can't believe I'm standing in front of the Prince of Darkness completely unprepared, wearing vomit-green furry PJ bottoms, Grinch slippers, and a flimsy T-shirt with no bra underneath that I used as a napkin all afternoon.

Tristan clears his throat.

"What—how—why are you here?" I stammer, folding my arms across my chest.

He shrugs, shaking snow from his boots. "Dylan invited me. My flight got canceled, so we drove up together instead."

That's when the idiot himself enters the house with a boastful, "Merry Christmas."

Dylan is greeted only by a frosty atmosphere and tense quiet.

"Hey, Dylan." It takes effort not to grind my teeth. "Can we talk in private for a second?"

My brother stares between me and his best friend and rolls his eyes, but he still nods, following me upstairs to my bedroom.

5

TRISTAN

There is nothing private about Nina's conversation with her brother. As I lean against the cool wall of the Thompsons' entryway, the chaos of the confrontation echoes down the stairs as loud as if I were in the room with them.

"You really had to invite him, didn't you? Of all people!" Nina shouts, her voice dripping with venom. I can almost picture her vibrant green eyes flashing with anger as she delivers one insult after another. Dylan's muffled replies are barely audible.

"If I wanted to spend my holidays with the Prince of Darkness, I'd have gone to a Black Sabbath reunion, not our living room!"

At least she's creative. I should probably be offended. But as I listen, I can't shake the image of Nina in that white T-shirt, the fabric leaving nothing to the imagination. That image, along with the memory of her unexpected reveal the other night, lingers uncomfortably in my mind, painting every curve and shadow of her fit body in vivid detail. It's a mental picture I have no business entertaining, not about my best friend's little sister. But it's there, taking center stage in my thoughts. Has been for a couple of days now.

"Insufferable jerk," Nina spits out, her words hitting me like a series of tiny punches.

"Ah, come on now, sis," Dylan counters, his voice briefly rising above the fray. "He's not that bad."

"Right," I mutter under my breath, rolling my eyes. My gaze slides over to a framed family photo on the wall—a much younger Nina stares back, hair a frizzy mess, jug ears sticking out from beneath. She must've been about that age when I first met her, a tiny whimsical pest, for sure. But she's no gremlin now.

Two nights ago, watching her stare right into my eyes, bold as she dropped that wretched towel, has re-wired my brain. I can no longer see her only as Dylan's younger sister. At present, she's filed away as a hot-as-fuck woman who happens to hate my guts.

I drag a hand over my face. Maybe coming here was a mistake. I should've stayed in New York. Work. I try not to be sentimental about Christmas. But Dylan insisted so much. He couldn't stand the thought of me abandoned in our apartment for the holidays. And so I came.

"No. No!" Nina's protests keep ricocheting down the stairs. "You brought Satan himself to our doorstep. What's next, a holiday dinner with the Four Horsemen of the Apocalypse?"

I wince, sorry that Dylan has to take the heat for inviting me over. Nina sounds even more aggravated than usual by my presence. She'll make us both pay for it. If anyone can hold a grudge, it's Nina Thompson.

My thoughts scatter as Mr. Thompson appears in the hallway, his genial smile undeterred by the cacophony above us. "Thought I heard someone come in." He greets me, extending his arm. The sound of Nina's ongoing tirade lends a bizarre soundtrack to our handshake.

"Hey, Mr. Thompson." I clutch his hand. "Good to see you."

"Please, call me Greg," he insists, as always. "You're practically family."

"Thanks, Greg." I try to sound grateful, but it's hard to focus on pleasantries with Nina's verbal assault still going strong upstairs.

As her voice crescendos with a creative string of insults aimed at me, Mr. Thompson winces playfully. "Ah, are those my daughter's dulcet tones?" he quips, the corner of his mouth twitching in amusement.

I can't help but chuckle, even as Nina's verbal daggers keep flying down the stairs. "She certainly has a way with words," I admit.

"Always has, ever since she was little," her dad reminisces, a twinkle in his eye. "I remember when she argued with her kindergarten teacher about the correct pronunciation of 'tomato.'"

"Sounds like Nina, alright." I nod, trying to picture a pint-sized version of her standing up to authority with the same fiery determination she shows me.

Mr. Thompson tries to reply but is stopped short by Nina's increasingly agitated tones.

"Christmas is a celebration about Jesus being born, and you literally brought the Antichrist in a business suit into our house. You're forcing us to spend the best time of the year with the man who probably inspired every villain in holiday movies. What, was the Grinch too busy?"

Mr. Thompson jokingly lowers the corners of his mouth and tilts his head as if to say, impressive.

I shrug. "Guess I can add holiday villain to my resume now."

"Next to Antichrist in a suit," he quips. "I'd say you're moving ahead, young man."

I glimpse Mrs. Thompson's reflection in the hallway mirror just before Lisa enters the hall, her brow furrowed with concern as she takes in the commotion. "What on Earth is all this noise about?"

she asks, her eyes darting between me and the stairs. Embarrassment colors her cheeks as Nina's rampage continues, but she doesn't let it affect her composure.

"Tristan, dear, it's so wonderful to have you with us again."

Her warm welcome instantly makes me feel at ease despite the chaos.

"Thank you, Mrs. Thompson. It's great to be here," I reply, returning her smile. Her presence has always had a calming effect on me, even now amid Nina's tornado-like outbursts.

"Please, call me Lisa," she insists, as she's done countless times before. I nod, same as I did with Mr. Thompson.

"Excuse me for a moment, will you?" Dylan's mom eyes the staircase with determination. "I need to speak with my daughter."

"Of course," I respond, watching as she gracefully ascends the stairs.

As she reaches the top, she puts an end to the argument, her voice carrying sufficient authority to make even the most stubborn of children listen.

"Nina!" she calls out firmly. "Enough with the shouting! This is not how we treat guests, especially not one who's been a friend of the family for so long."

Instead of being subdued, Nina yells even louder. "Did you know about this?"

"Of course I knew."

"Then why didn't you tell me?"

"Because your father and I didn't want to spend the morning hearing you complain. And I'd hoped you'd be more mature about it."

"But Mom, he—" she starts, only to be cut off.

"No 'buts,' young lady. You will apologize to Tristan and behave yourself for the rest of his visit. Is that clear?" Mrs. Thompson's voice is unwavering, leaving no room for argument.

"If he stays, I go!"

"Nowhere to go, darling, we're snowed in."

"I hope you're happy," Nina yells, presumably at Dylan. Then a door slams.

My best friend hops back down the stairs next, a sheepish expression on his face. "Don't worry, man, she'll get over it."

I seriously doubt it, but, as Mrs. Thompson pointed out, we are snowed in. Dylan and I barely made it here. I couldn't go back to New York even if I wanted to—at least not tonight.

* * *

Nina seems to vanish off the face of the Earth for the next hour, leaving behind only the echo of her outrage. I contemplate the possibility of clearing the air between us, but who am I kidding? Nina Thompson and peace talks go together like oil and water. I drop the silly idea, focusing instead on the warmth of the Thompson household—a sheer contrast to the coldness and disinterest I'm used to at home.

Two days ago, the night I found Nina and her roommates in my apartment, my mom had just informed me with a two-sentence text that they were canceling Christmas as they wouldn't be home for the holidays. Adding a short "see you next year" at the end of the message. Hard to say if she meant it as in "see you in a few days in the new year" or as in "see you next Christmas." Probably the latter.

I'm not even sure why I still bother to buy tickets to go home when it's clear my parents couldn't care less. Even without JFK shutting down, I would've been stranded for the holidays regardless.

But at least the storm has provided me with an excuse to give people as to why I'm spending Christmas with my best friend's family and not mine. I don't need anyone's sympathy or to be pitied. Especially not by a certain green-eyed, sharp-tongued beauty, who regards me as a particularly distasteful bug.

Nursing my second mug of hot chocolate Mrs. Thompson insisted I have, I stare at the blizzard raging outside, feeling slightly guilty that I'm glad about the horrible weather. The gale really came as the perfect excuse to spend Christmas with a family who actually cherishes the holidays and appreciates being together. A family whose members love each other. And even if I'm public enemy number one for a certain member of the household, it's still better than being persona non grata for everyone back home.

I haven't even asked my parents where they've gone off to. Each new rejection hurts a little less. Maybe I'll become immune soon.

From a young age—too early for any kid to draw that conclusion—I realized they'd never wanted the bother of taking care of a child. I was raised by nannies until they could ship me off to boarding school and be rid of me altogether. The jury's still out on whether I was a planned addition to the family they thought would be less troublesome or an unwanted mistake.

Anyway, my Christmases in this house with Dylan and his family are the happiest I remember. And I'm sorry Nina loathes having me here. I honestly have no plans to make this forced cohabitation any more difficult for her than it needs to be. I'll be a good boy this year; no teasing or riling her up.

I take another sip of chocolate and vow to lay down my arms. I'll just stay out of her way as much as possible and quit fueling whatever stupid feud has been going on between us.

As another hour rolls in, with still no signs of Nina emerging from wherever she's holed up, I decide it's high time to unpack. That's when I realize my suitcase isn't where I left it in my room. I call it "my room" because it's the room where I always sleep when I visit Dylan. Incidentally, it is also the room next to Nina's. A circumstance that has never bothered me before, but now, the idea of her lying on a bed just a drywall away is... troublesome for reasons I will not explore.

As is the disappearance of my suitcase.

A sweep of the house confirms that my bag is nowhere to be found. I can't shake a growing suspicion that little Miss Grinch had something to do with the sudden MIA baggage. I look everywhere a second time, and when I still can't find it, I knock on her door.

She opens, eyes glaring. I have an instant to assess that she's changed into a cozy knitted sweater that hugs her figure, and dark leggings that sculpt her long, lean legs before the door slams back in my face.

Well, at least she was covered up this time. If I didn't know better, I'd say she'd even made an effort.

"Nina." I bang on her door again, all my good intentions to keep calm and not engage with her already forgotten. "I need to change."

The door reopens, and she leans on the threshold, casually checking her nails, an infuriating smirk curling the corners of her mouth.

Have her lips always been this red and pouty?

"Calling me Nina, uh? Did you misplace your pitchfork?"

I don't know why, but I can't get myself to call her Gremlin anymore. Not after what her roommate said the other night about the joke not being funny if I'm the only one laughing. I still haven't puzzled out why the name has gotten so offensive to her, but the hurt I saw flash in Nina's eyes when I asked for my towel back and called her Gremlin stayed with me, impossible to forget. That brief flicker of pain kept me awake all night. Well, that and the memory of her long legs, luscious curves, and round—*I need to stop!*

Now's not the time to get soft—or worse, randy. I've vowed not to provoke her, but that doesn't mean I'm just going to let her roll all over me. Even if I could imagine a few scenarios where her rolling over me wouldn't be half bad. And I shouldn't. Argh, what is wrong with me?

I tug at my cashmere sweater. "I want to get out of these clothes."

Nina's eyes drop to my chest, and when her gaze lifts back to mine, something is stirring behind the icy glares.

"Don't get too excited," she quips. "It's not a full moon yet."

I ignore the way the word excited coming out of that suddenly irresistible, pouty mouth makes me feel. Yeah, not touching that. "Where did you put my suitcase?"

She looks at her nails again and shrugs. "Try searching in the shadows; I hear that's where you do your best work."

Okay, she's not going to let it go. Message clear. No truce is possible. It's an all-out war.

My jaw sets. "If this is how you want to do it."

Her eyes flash, but she keeps quiet.

I rake a hand through my hair. Think, Tristan. Where could she have put the suitcase? Nowhere in the house. At least, not in a place I've already checked. And I've looked *everywhere*. Twice.

How else can I find my bag? Did she leave the house unnoticed, bring it somewhere?

I have my iPad in there. Under Nina's amused gaze, I whip out my phone and check the geotag. But the localization only confirms the suitcase is here somewhere. I could call myself on Skype. Worth a shot.

I open the app and dial my tablet handle. The line connects, but I can't hear the ringtone from here. My bag is not upstairs or stashed away in the attic.

Ignoring Nina, I head downstairs. Just as I reach the bottom of the stairs, a faint ringing becomes audible. I turn to the kitchen, but the sound turns muffled, same when I try the living room.

With a horrifying realization, I open the front door. Drifts of snow attack me, snowflakes blowing in my face and into my mouth, but the ringtone becomes louder. I follow the faint melody into the storm, wading through knee-deep snow until I discover a rectangular-shaped hole in the white mantle where my suitcase is already submerged by a fresh powdery blanket.

I'd laugh if I didn't want to cry.

Already half-frozen to death, I plod the last of the distance and retrieve the suitcase from the ground. At least it was a rigid casing and nothing should've gotten wet.

Shivering, I lug the case behind me, trudging for the heat of the house.

I stagger back inside, leaving a trail of half-melted deluge. My fingers are numb, barely able to latch onto the handle to close the front door.

As the hot indoor air hits my frozen extremities, the skin on my hands and face burns, making me almost regret the anesthetized sensation of a few moments ago. Feeling like a mix between a ball of fire and ice, I drag the suitcase up the stairs.

Nina is still there, leaning against the doorframe of her room.

She smirks, her eyes lighting up with mischief. "Find everything okay out there, Tristan?"

I glare at her, my cold, wet misery a stark contrast to her warm, smug confidence. "Thanks for showing me the rolling in the snow facilities," I retort as I shake flakes from my hair like a dog after a bath, sending droplets scattering across the hallway. "Care to show me where the sauna is?"

I relish her wince as beads of melted snow land on her pretty face.

She tosses her head, her blonde hair flipping dismissively as she wipes away the moisture with a flick of her wrist. "Oh, the sauna? That's reserved for guests who don't sign their Christmas cards with 'Best Malevolent Wishes,'" Nina teases, her voice laced with feigned innocence.

With a sly grin, I consider my next move. She's looking at me with that defiant tilt to her chin, daring me to up the ante. If she wants to play, I can play. "I'll just have to find other ways to thaw then," I say, my tone subtly coaxing.

Her cheeks flush. Good to know she rattles.

Nina pushes off the doorframe, all haughty indifference. "Enjoy your frozen change of clothes." Then, that incandescent green gaze drops to my nether regions. "I hope nothing shrivels."

And the way she looks back up at me, a little suggestively and with a satisfied, impudent smirk, has the opposite effect of shriveling *anything* down there.

6

NINA

Revenge is coming. I sense it in Tristan's exaggerated graciousness as he offers me the bread basket during dinner. Or in the attentive way he pours me water, asking, "Ice?"

"I can take it myself, thank you."

"No need." He grabs the ice tongs and drops three cubes in my glass, tortuously slow. They look only half-made—too small—but still clink loudly as they fall into the glass. Each chink reverberates against my spine.

Tristan looks at me, blue eyes so deep and clear they could belong to a glacier. His beauty is undeniable, the kind that could easily grace the covers of magazines or make an entire room fall silent as he walks in. Dark hair, the color of midnight, falls effortlessly around a face chiseled from alabaster, providing a stark contrast that only accentuates the intensity in those eyes that seem to hold the world's secrets.

He's a work of art.

But I see past the facade, into the shadows lurking beneath the surface of his perfect features. It's in the way his gaze holds mine, intense and unyielding as if he's peering into my very soul, searching for something he can twist and bend—hurt, his specialty. His appearance is a deception, a mask so beautifully crafted that it's almost impossible to discern the darkness that dwells underneath. And yet, I can feel it, a cold undercurrent that whispers of danger, reminding me that even the most exquisite roses have thorns.

I tap my foot under the table, wondering what he has planned to get back at me for hiding his suitcase. I know he has something in store. This kindness is just a provocation. One more polite gesture, and I'm going to lose it and scream. I glare at him, my nerves tangling into knots.

"Relax, Nina," Mom says, piling mashed potatoes onto my plate. "You look like you're about to jump out of your skin."

"I'm fine," I mutter, darting a glance at Tristan. He grins at me, and I scowl. Jerk.

As we eat, my eyes follow Tristan's every move, waiting for the other shoe to drop. My phone buzzes in my pocket and I grab it, my pulse quickening when I see the sender. A text from Tristan.

THE PRINCE OF DARKNESS

You look lovely when you're paranoid ;)

Lovely. The word washes over me like warm honey, unexpected, sweet, and annoyingly sticky. It's ridiculous, really, how a single positive adjective from him can send such conflicting signals through my body. Part of me—the part that's hated him for what feels like an eternity—wants to toss my phone right at his smug face. But there's this other part, a traitorous, whisper-thin sliver of my consciousness that flutters at the compliment, however backhanded it might be.

I scowl, trying to shake off the absurd fluttering in my stomach. It's Tristan, for crying out loud. The same guy who's made it his mission to make my life a living hell every chance he gets. And yet, here I am, caught in the crossfire of my tumultuous feelings, hating how my heart skips a beat when another speech bubble appears underneath the first text.

But seconds tick by, and no new texts come through.

I glance up from under my eyelashes to find Tristan fumbling with his phone under the table, a frown creasing his forehead.

Come on, I think impatiently. What's taking so long?

I shift in my seat, checking my screen again, but the speech bubbles continue to mock me, moving but unchanging. I stare at Tristan, willing him to look up. But he remains focused on his phone, oblivious to my inner turmoil. I'm half tempted to snatch the darn thing from his hands to see what he's writing, but that would be too desperate even for me.

The clank of silverware against plates fills the air as we continue with our dinner. My parents and Dylan are talking, but I'm unable to concentrate on the conversation or the food in front of me. The speech bubbles on my phone screen are like a persistent echo in an empty room, impossible to silence. Their constant bubbling is gnawing at my insides and threatening to make me lose my mind.

That's when I notice Tristan has put his phone away and is scarfing down Mom's roast with gusto. I stare at my screen again. The speech bubbles are still there. But if he's not typing anymore... I frown. Am I out of signal? No, I have full bars. So why isn't his message coming through? With the time he took, Tristan must've written a poem. Is my phone broken? I shake it, then tap on the screen. The speech bubble opens up as an image attachment. The jerk has sent me a GIF. He wasn't typing anything.

When I look up, Tristan is watching me, a smug smirk on his face. He winks.

I bite the inside of my cheek, my mind a whirlwind of irritation, confusion, and an inexplicable respect. That was an admittedly good prank. With a huff, I shove the phone back into my pocket. Let him preen, think he's won. I won't give him the satisfaction of seeing me ruffled.

In need of a respite, I reach for my glass and take a drink. The water glides down my throat, soothing, until my eyes cross over a dark shape swirling in the liquid.

A scream claws its way up my windpipe, shattering the comfortable hum of dinner. The glass slips from my grasp, water sloshing down my front, icy rivulets snaking through my clothes as panic and disgust war for dominance.

"Honey, are you alright?" My dad pats me between the shoulder blades as I cough out more water.

"There's a bug in my water!" I gasp out, my voice hitching, as every pair of eyes at the table snaps toward me.

My mom is up in an instant, concern etched in her features. "A bug? In the dead of winter, honey?"

"It's in my glass!" I point, my hand trembling, only to watch in mounting horror as my dad fishes out the offending object with a spoon.

He inspects it, then chuckles, holding it out for me to see. "Nina, it's just a raisin."

A raisin. Not a bug. My cheeks flame with embarrassment. How did a raisin get in my glass?

My scalp prickles and I turn my head to find Tristan's gaze locked on me. He's trying to stifle a laugh, unsuccessfully, his shoulders are shaking with silent mirth.

Our eyes meet, and in his, I recognize a glimmer of triumph. Oh, I see, this was his play all along. The showcase of politeness was just to gain access to my food and water supply. The text message was a diversion to lull me into a false sense of security before the major attack. He knows I hate bugs and that I freak out even for the smallest midge.

I narrow my eyes at him. He merely raises his glass in a mock toast, that infuriating smirk never leaving his face.

I'm soaked, embarrassed, and now more determined than ever. I push back from the table, hands balled into fists at my sides. "You're dead, Montgomery," I hiss on my way to change.

His grin only widens. "Promises, promises."

I storm away before I do something I regret, like punch that infuriating smirk right off his face. In my room, I peel off my wet sweater and use it to towel off.

After I've changed into dry clothes, there's a knock at my door. I throw it open, ready to tear into Tristan, but it's my brother on the other side.

"I come in peace," Dylan says, hands raised.

I cross my arms, eyebrow lifting skeptically. "What do you want?"

"To make sure you're not planning to murder my best friend." Dylan pushes past me into the room.

"No promises," I mutter darkly.

My brother sits on the edge of my bed. "Come on, Nina. It was just a harmless prank. And I'm sure you've started it somehow."

I purse my lips, neither confirming nor denying.

"Promise me you won't go crazy and ruin Christmas for everyone," Dylan says.

"You've already ruined Christmas by bringing Malefico here."

Dylan scolds me with a reproachful stare.

"Fine." I flop onto my bed next to him with a huff. "I won't kill him."

"Or maim him," Dylan adds, only half joking. "Or publicly humiliate him."

"I get the picture," I grumble.

Dylan reaches out and squeezes my shoulder. "Atta girl. Now

let's go back downstairs. Uncle Milo, Agatha, Eric, and the kids are coming over for Charades night."

Milo is Dad's brother. Agatha, his daughter. And Eric, her husband. They have two kids, Teddy, three, and Zoe, nine.

I raise an eyebrow. "They're coming even in this weather?"

"They live too close for a little blizzard to stop them. And it's Charades night."

"Do I have to play?"

"Yes." Dylan nods. "Mandatory family fun. They'll be here soon."

As if on cue, the doorbell rings.

"I don't want to go."

"Come on. You know Teddy will cry all night if he doesn't see you." He pats my shoulder. "And Zoe will have no cool role model."

I roll my eyes. "Flattery doesn't work on me."

Dylan hardly suppresses a smirk. "Oh, I think it does." He stands up and offers me a hand.

I let him pull me up and follow him out of my room, bracing myself for an entire night of having to stare at Tristan Montgomery's smug face.

7

NINA

As I stomp downstairs after my brother, rage against the unwanted houseguest resurfaces, bubbling inside me with every step. How dare he ruin the best time of the year? I usually love Charades night, but not when I have to share my family with him.

At the bottom of the stairs, loud voices come from the kitchen. Uncle Milo and his family must've gone in for a taste of Mom's famous pecan pie. Wanting an extra minute of quiet, I deviate to the living room.

A poor choice. As I enter the room, I find Tristan alone in there, leaning against the fireplace, one arm braced over the mantel, staring into the crackling fire. With the flickering flames illuminating his beautiful features in a dance of light and shadows, his cheekbones seem sharper, his jaw even more defined, and his eyes an unsettled storm that threatens to knock the wind out of me. I shake off the unwanted admiration and march up to him.

"You," I snarl, pointing an accusing finger at him. "I know it was you."

He glances at me, eyes glinting with satisfaction. The smug curl of his lips makes it clear he's been awaiting my reaction. "Know *what* was me?"

"The raisin. In my water glass. You put it there somehow."

He arches a brow. "Oh, is that what all the fuss was about, a raisin? You scare easily, Thompson."

"Don't play dumb with me, *Montgomery*." I jab his chest with my finger—bad idea. I almost chip a fingernail on the solid wall of muscles. "I know your tricks. How did you do it? There's no way it was in there when you poured in the water."

A chuckle rumbles in his chest. "In the water? No, you're right."

He stares at me intensely. I might have melted under someone else's gaze, but his unapologetic blue stare is as infuriating as it is captivating, and still allows my brain cogs to turn. "You mean it was in the *ice*? But..." I scowl at him as comprehension dawns, anger battling with reluctant admiration for the cunning simplicity of his prank. "You froze it in an ice cube, didn't you? Like a slow time-release bomb. That's why the ice was only half done."

He gives a noncommittal shrug, the picture of innocence.

Am I imagining it, or is there a glint of something more than just amusement in his blue eyes?

Before I can argue or speculate further, Mom comes into the living room, carrying the Charades box. She rattles it as a makeshift call to arms.

Tristan pushes off the mantel, coming close enough for me to feel the heat of his body, a silent reminder he's always there, watching and waiting to strike again.

"This isn't over," I mutter under my breath.

A soft chuckle in my ear sends a tingle zipping up my spine. "Where would the fun be otherwise?"

Tristan goes to sit on the couch next to Dylan, but I stay close to the fireplace, needing the extra warmth after the chills the Prince of Darkness sent down my arms.

The rest of the family slowly files into the living room. Uncle Milo, first, then Agatha with Teddy in her arms. Zoe barrels into me with the enthusiasm only a nine-year-old can muster, nearly knocking me over into the hearth. I catch myself and laugh, pulling her into a hug.

I give Agatha a much more mature kiss on the cheeks as we squeeze a delighted Teddy between us. The toddler is still laughing as Eric comes closer to ruffle my hair in that brotherly way he picked up from Dylan when they became fast friends. The room fills with laughter and the warmth of family.

"Alright, folks, time to pick teams!" Mom announces with her signature school teacher authority no one dares to challenge.

Everyone settles somewhere on the floor or perched on furniture. Mom passes around the satchel for us to put our names in. The black velvet sack, soft and slightly worn at the seams, has been a silent witness to many holiday cheers and family squabbles. We each take a turn, scribbling our names on slips of paper, folding them into secretive little squares, and dropping them into the depths of the small bag. The anticipation is palpable, as alliances are about to be forged and rivalries momentarily set aside.

The room hushes as Mom, with a dramatic flourish, begins to draw names. "Team One," she announces, her voice echoing with the weight of ceremony. "Uncle Milo..." A cheer goes up from the corner where Uncle Milo sits, his wooly ugly sweater a riot of festive colors. "Agatha..." My cousin gives a little wave, her grin bright. "Nina..." I nod, keeping a pleasant smile on my face, hoping my competitive edge isn't already showing, even as I inwardly cringe. Uncle Milo is the worst at party games, especially Charades. I really didn't want him on my team.

My stomach knots as Mom's hand delves into the satchel again. We can't have another poor player. I want Dylan. "Tristan," she calls out instead.

The name hangs in the air, a cruel fate I can't escape. I turn to look at him, our eyes locking in a silent acknowledgment of the unexpected twist. His grin is infuriatingly confident. He'd better back up all that cockiness with a degree in miming. Already being on the same team with Tristan feels like being asked to dance with a cobra—dangerous and sleazy. I don't need him to also be a lousy player.

I suppress a curse. Now I can't even hope to blow his team to smithereens with my superior Charades skills. Instead, I'm shackled to him, our victory dependent on mutual cooperation. The irony isn't lost on me, nor is the fact that this might be Mom's subtle way of forcing a holiday truce. I've suspected her of cheating at team-picking for years. Of course, I have no proof nor any idea how she could do it.

"Play nice, you two," Dylan warns, his protective big brother's gaze flitting between us.

I smile viciously brightly. "I'd worry more about not having my ass handed to me if I were you." I mimic an L on my forehead.

Before Dylan can reply, Dad claps his hands, eyes alight with enthusiasm. "Excellent! The teams are set. Who wants to go first?"

"We will pick by chance like we always do, *Greg*," my mom scolds him. She drops the names back into the satchel and picking one out, announces, "Tristan, you mimic first."

I suppress an inner groan. Despite the swagger, he probably sucks, and we have zero chances of winning.

The Prince of Darkness picks up his card and stands in the middle of the room. As soon as Mom turns the hourglass, he pretends to crank an old-fashioned movie camera.

"Movie," Agatha shouts.

Tristan nods.

Before even telling us how many words are in the title, Tristan starts punching the air.

"*Creed*," Agatha guesses.

Tristan waves past his shoulder as if to say older.

"*Kung Fu Panda*?" I ask.

He vehemently shakes his head while still fighting an invisible opponent. Is he trying to actively sabotage us?

"Well, don't just stand there like that punching at nothing," I snap. "Mimic something else."

Tristan gives me a scathing look but stops the kickboxing work-out. He thinks for a second and then mimics pulling on a cord as if to sound a bell.

We all watch him, perplexed.

"*Selling Sunset*?" I venture. Those gals surely don't pull punches and they ring lots of bells.

Tristan scolds me as if meaning *not even close*. Yeah, that's a TV show—my bad. He's throwing me off my game. Agatha and I stare at each other, then at Uncle Milo, who only raises his hands, saying, "I'm a pacifist."

And then time runs out. We lost our first point.

"It was *Rocky*," Tristan declares.

I'm not sure how I would've mimed that, but it surely would've been better. I draw in a long inhale, trying to keep my cool as we continue the game. The rounds pass in a blur of laughter and confusion. Each team takes its turn, the air thick with competitive tension and the occasional cheer when guesses hit the mark. I struggle to concentrate on the game as the awareness of Tristan's proximity tugs at the edges of my focus, an unwelcome distraction.

Our eyes meet for a brief moment, inciting a mix of frustration and attraction. He's always been able to get under my skin.

"Okay, it's your turn, Nina!" Dylan announces, bringing me back to the present.

I draw a card from the pile, *The Sound of Music*. Excitement rushes through me. This one should be easy enough to enact.

I signal it's a movie. Even Uncle Milo can guess this part by now. Then make a four with my fingers to signal the title is four words and a two to signify that I'm starting with the second word.

Keeping my hair down because I'm still standing before the Prince of Darkness, I cup my hand behind my ear, a universal sign for listening or sound.

"Ear!" Teddy shouts, and I shake my head.

I keep cupping my ear, but no one guesses anything. Oh, screw Tristan and his mocking, I pull my hair behind my ear and fully cup it in a listening gesture, pointing at what goes inside, hoping they'll get it's sound.

But I'm promptly rewarded for showing vulnerability when Tristan confidently calls out, "Elephant!"

The room falls silent for a split second. The word looms over our heads, heavy with implication. My blood boils, making my cheeks flame with embarrassment. The playful atmosphere suddenly transforms into a pressure cooker of emotions for me. I can't take it anymore. Years of grievances and mocking bubble to the surface.

"Really, Tristan? Elephant?" I glare at him, unable to contain my anger. "What movie did you have in mind with Elephants?"

"*Water for Elephants*?" He seems taken aback by my reaction.

"That's a three-word title, and I was mimicking a four-word one and I specified it was the second word."

"No, you're right, sorry, keep going."

"Why? So you can make fun of my ears some more? You might've as well guessed *Dumbo*."

"What?" His jaw drops. "Wait, Nina, that's not what I—" Tristan tries to explain, his eyes widening with surprise.

But all I can hear is the rush of blood to my head and the echo of Tristan's mocking guess.

"Save it, Tristan," I snap, cutting him off. "I'm sick of your little jabs and constant teasing."

"Guys, come on, let's just calm down and finish the game," Dylan interjects, attempting to defuse the situation.

But my mind is racing, replaying every snarky comment and hurtful joke Tristan has made over the years. I feel like no one truly understands how cruel he can be, and I refuse to be his punching bag any longer.

"Look, Nina, I wasn't trying to make fun of you," Tristan insists, his expression a blend of exasperation and concern. "I genuinely thought your clue was about an elephant."

"Right, because mimicking listening clearly means 'elephant,'" I retort sarcastically. My blood continues to boil, burning a path through my veins as I remember thirteen-year-old me, crushed in a corner and crying after he mocked my ears.

Tristan still looks shocked, his mouth opening and closing as if he's searching for the right thing to say. "I—I genuinely didn't mean it like that. I just said the first thing that came to mind."

"I don't believe you. You always do this," I accuse, my voice rising with each word. "You always have to make it personal, don't you?"

"Come on, Nina," Mom chimes in, "you're overreacting. I'm sure Tristan didn't mean anything by it."

"Overreacting?" My stomach twists into a pretzel of annoyance, except this one has been soaked in gasoline and set on fire. I clench my fists. "This isn't some isolated incident. He's been tormenting me for years!"

"Okay, everyone just needs to take a deep breath," Dylan suggests, rubbing his forehead with his fingers. My brother is trying to mediate, but all I want is for someone, anyone, to recognize that Tristan is acting in bad faith.

"Maybe you should've taken a breath before you invited Satan over for Christmas," I accuse.

"Nina, stop!" Mom yells. "I haven't raised you to be rude to our guests."

"Fine!" I exclaim, stomping away. "You all enjoy your precious game night. I'm going to my room."

As I march away, I feel their eyes following me, judging and whispering. I'm aware of how petulant and childish I must seem, but I can't bring myself to care. Not when every part of me is screaming to get away, to find a space where I can breathe, where I don't have to face Tristan or his cutting jokes.

Nobody seems to understand how Dylan's best friend has made it his life's mission to hound me. But I won't stick around for another serving of his ridicule, not this time. I'm done.

"Wait, Nina," Tristan calls out, but I ignore him and continue my march to the sanctuary of my bedroom. I slam the door shut, and finally, tears prick at the corners of my eyes. One thing is certain—he's going to pay for this.

8

TRISTAN

As the house settles into a deep silence, its tranquility is a stark contrast to the storm brewing in my lungs. When I exit the bathroom after brushing my teeth, I linger outside Nina's shut door. The wooden panels seem to stare at me accusingly.

Great, now even inanimate objects are judging me.

I glare back. *I didn't mean it*, I want to yell.

Dylan passes me by on the way to his room and, taking in my guilty look, says, "Leave it, man. She'll get over it."

Easy for him to say. He's not the one who mortally offended his sister.

I give him a nod, but I can't shake off the night's events—the Charades fiasco, especially. Why did I have to guess elephant when she acted out big ears? Even if she meant sound, that still looked like a pachyderm imitation to me. I genuinely didn't want to gall Nina, but the hurt in her eyes, that wounded pride, it claws at me. Same as a cat to a new sofa—unrelenting and leaving a mark.

After Dylan disappears into his room, I let out a sigh and my shoulders slump. Maybe it would be wiser to leave this until morning, but my feet stay rooted in front of Nina's door as if they've made their own decision.

Compelled by this inexplicable mix of guilt and the recent, irresistible pull I feel toward her, I raise my hand, hesitating for a moment before softly knocking on her door.

Gosh, what am I, a lovesick teenager?

I don't even know what I'm hoping for. For a chance to explain? To apologize? Sadly, I'm granted neither. Only silence greets me back, the barrier between us more than just physical.

"Nina?" I try, half-expecting the door to open and for a book to fly through and hit me square in the face.

But nothing.

I sigh, whispering an apology into the void. "I'm sorry." The words feel as heavy as the air around me, laden with remorse and a building sense of longing that complicates everything.

Still no response. I drop the flat of my palm on the door, the weight of our unresolved tension as tangible as the wood beneath my fingertips.

After a few more moments of sharp silence, I give up. But as I retreat to my room, my mind still races. The quiet of the night amplifies every thought, every what-if. I sit on the bed and stare at the wall I share with Nina. Knowing that her headboard is on the other side does little to ease my nerves. It's a cruel reminder of the physical closeness and emotional distance that now defines us.

Sleep is a battle tonight. I toss and turn, then lie flat on my back. The room is dark, but my eyes are wide open, tracing the familiar shapes of the furniture like negatives in a photograph. It's as if I'm waiting for something, anticipating some sign that she might forgive me or at least acknowledge my existence. Finally, my body gives in to exhaustion and I start to drift off.

Just as I'm about to surrender to the weary darkness, a shrill beep pierces the stillness. Groggily, I fumble around on the night-stand, expecting to find my phone, but my hand closes over a small, cold object. It's a Casio watch, its face glowing mockingly in the dark.

Confusion turns to irritation as I flip on the night light and silence the timepiece. Dylan's dad notoriously collects these watches, but he keeps them in a cabinet in his studio. Unless they've grown legs and developed a taste for midnight strolls, there's no way the Casio ended up here by mistake. A prank? A watch going off in the middle of the night feels like a deliberate jab. *Subtle, Nina. Very subtle.* I stare daggers at the wall behind me.

"Seriously?" I mutter, tossing the vintage chronometer on the carpet.

The watch lands with a soft thud. I feel a momentary pang of guilt for mistreating Mr. Thompson's collection. But, honestly, he has only his daughter to thank for any mishandling of his watches. I mean, she weaponized them against me.

I pinch the bridge of my nose. That woman.

I settled back down under the covers. Once again wide awake. Mind churning.

At least she's not ignoring me? Silver linings, Tristan.

I'm not even sure if I'm more irritated she's retaliating or glad. Barely an hour later, I have my answer as a second alarm shatters the quiet.

This time, I'm on my feet, scanning the room with bleary eyes. The sound leads me to the bookshelf, where another watch is wedged between two novels, its beep taunting me from the shadows. I read the titles on the spines: *Paradise Lost* by John Milton and Bram Stoker's *Dracula*. Of course, she'd pick an epic poem featuring Satan as a central character and a classic tale with a bloodsucking monster as a protagonist. Nina is more hammer than feather when making a point.

"This is child's play," I grumble, although there's a part of me that admires the ingenuity and ruthlessness of her plan. Note to self: Never underestimate a woman with a bone to pick. Especially if that woman is Nina Thompson and the grievance is with me.

The third alarm at 2 a.m. has me questioning my sanity and Nina's. We're officially in a Casio Cold War. It takes me a while to locate the source this time. The beeping comes from inside the closet, muffled underneath a pile of blankets. As I dig through the mess, I find the watch, its alarm relentless. "Okay, Nina, game on," I sigh, the challenge clear, even if the hour is ungodly.

She wants the gloves to come off? I can take them off. And to think of all the time I wasted feeling sorry for her tonight or guilty. I shouldn't have. Nina Thompson is a force of chaos, a whirlwind of revenge, and it's impossible for me not to feel a twinge of pride at her boldness. She's like a tiny, angry Fury come straight out of a Greek mythology book. A deity of vengeance who punishes crimes hidden in a gorgeous female body.

Despite the hour and the sleep that I'm not getting, there's an odd sense of exhilaration in this silent war between us.

By the time four thirty rolls around, I've found two more Casio watches. One taped under the desk, a spot I only discovered after minutes of confused searching. And the other directly under my pillow. *Not the kind of pillow talk I'm interested in.*

I'm impressed and infuriated in equal measure. "She's outdone herself," I admit through gritted teeth, the realization that I'm losing this silent battle settling in.

I retrieve the last watch just before dawn breaks. When I find it tucked inside my shoe, I shake my head in disbelief, exhaustion tugging at me. Still, as I collapse onto the bed, wonderment seeps into my bones. That she's gone through so much trouble to get back at me shows, even if in a twisted way, that she cares.

Maybe not how I want her to, but it's something. Full-blown

hatred is better than indifference. It means I still know how to push her buttons. And I'm not sure why, but this Christmas I don't seem able to keep my hands off the console.

9

NINA

The next morning, I perch at the breakfast table, drumming my fingers, anticipation bubbling in my belly like a pot left on the stove. I'm eager to see how Tristan will react to my alarm clock vendetta.

I should be livid at him for what he said yesterday. But there's also something else wedged in my chest that I can't describe or comprehend. He put it there last night, as he stood outside my room whispering an apology. Munching on my toast, I reminisce about how hearing Tristan on the other side of my door rattled me. The soft knock that punched me in the solar plexus. The way he called my name as if it were a precious thing that might shatter if handled too roughly. That murmured *"I'm sorry."*

What's up with the decent person act?

"Morning," Dylan yawns as he enters the kitchen, joining me, Mom, and Dad. He seems surprised to find me already there. I'm notoriously not a morning person. "Hey, sis. You're up early."

I shrug, feigning nonchalance. "Couldn't sleep." Not even a lie. The plan was to keep the Prince of Darkness awake all night, but I couldn't help stirring, too, as I counted down the time to the next alarm, imagining his reaction, tensing in bed to hear any movement in the adjoining room.

Speaking of the devil... Tristan shuffles in a few minutes later, sleep-tousled but still impossibly gorgeous in gray sweatpants and a snug white T-shirt. Dark circles rim his eyes, and his hair sticks up in ten different directions.

I hide my smirk behind my coffee cup. Our eyes meet, a collision with blue fire that threatens to melt me into a puddle.

"Morning," he mumbles, grabbing the coffee pot.

"Good morning. Slept well?" I ask, the picture of innocence.

"Like a baby," he grunts, pouring a liberal amount of coffee into his mug and coming to sit next to me. Leaning close, he adds in a whisper, "I woke up every two hours and cried."

His warm breath brushes my neck, sending a shockwave of tingles cascading down my arms. The goosebumps worsen when our legs come in contact under the table. The side of his right thigh plastered against my left. Tristan doesn't move away. And, for unfathomable reasons, I don't retreat, either.

Seeing how everyone is abusing the caffeine today, Dad stands up and makes a new pot. The aroma of freshly brewed coffee fills the air, mingling with the scent of crispy bacon and golden-brown toast. I try my best to focus on the conversation between my parents, Dylan, and Tristan, but it's an uphill battle. The side of my thigh is slowly melting under the table. Tristan's leg feels scorching against mine. Who knew demons ran on hot blood?

Despite the distracting body contact, my mind is racing, attempting to anticipate what prank Tristan will pull on me as retaliation for the pleasant night of unrest I gifted him.

He's acting too casual. I'm sure he has something in store. Well, I've learned the hard way not to trust him with my drinks or food. I'm making an exception only for the pack of Oreos that we're sharing and only because he opened the tube in front of me. No occasion to tamper with it.

The cookies go untouched by everyone else in the house. Mom and Dad avoid them for health reasons, but Dylan just doesn't like them. I wonder how my brother turned out fine despite his poor taste in processed sweets.

I stuff another cookie in my mouth. I mean, they're delicious. How could any sane person not appreciate it?

"Nina." Dad pulls me back into the present. "Do you want a second cup of coffee, honey?"

I shake my head. "No, thanks. I'm good." If I ingest any more caffeine, my jitters are going to explode out of proportion.

Tristan's gaze flickers to me, amused. "You look preoccupied."

I shrug nonchalantly. "I'm peachy."

He arches an eyebrow but doesn't comment further.

Dylan looks between us suspiciously. "What's going on with you two?"

We both blink back at him like little angels, saying, "Nothing."

My brother doesn't look convinced. "So you patched things up after last night?"

Tristan drops an arm over my shoulders, pulling me close. "Yeah, your sister and I are all good now, aren't we, Nina?" His tone is playful, yet there's an underlying challenge in his eyes that only I can read. It negates everything he's saying, promising swift revenge.

But that's not even the most worrisome factor in this exchange. Right now, the lingering physical contact is my top concern. It sends ripples of unease through me, especially because I don't totally hate the weight of Tristan's arm on my shoulders. Or having more of his side pressed into me. He even smells good. A trace of spice mixing with clean soap, an intoxicating scent that whispers of temptation. After all, alluring innocent souls is his literal job.

"Yep, all g-great," I stammer.

Dylan's eyes narrow slightly, and I can tell he's not buying the charade for a second. "Right," he says, dragging out the word.

Tristan's arm is still around me when Dad changes the subject. "So, Tristan, how's that new software project coming along at your company?"

Tristan slides into business mode, the arm retreating from my shoulders as he turns to face my father. "It's going well, Mr. Thompson, Greg—" he corrects himself.

With a little more personal space available and an uninteresting subject being discussed, I'm free to tune them out once again. And go back to obsessing over what Tristan's next step is going to be.

He's acting freakishly calm. And, okay, waking him up every hour was admittedly mean, but he basically called me Dumbo. He deserved it.

As breakfast ends with no imaginary bugs crawling into my drink or sugar turning out to be salt in my morning coffee, I'm almost disappointed. Has Tristan decided to call a truce for real? It seems unlikely. I watch as he exits the kitchen, leaving me alone with my thoughts and the remnants of our meal.

In the Thompsons' strict organization of family chores, I always have to clear the breakfast table. Mostly because I've historically been the last to join and finish.

I collect the dirty dishes and rinse them in the sink before piling them into the dishwasher. I'm not one of those people willing to put everything in without a previous scrub and roll the dice to see what food scraps cling on like glitter after the wash cycle.

Uh, maybe my next prank for Tristan should be a glitter bomb. He'd never get rid of it. The iridescent dust would stick to him until he went to his grave. Which, with him, could be sooner than expected. I bet he sleeps in a coffin back at his place.

I let out a diabolical laugh in my mind as I imagine Tristan covered from head to toe in sparkly pink powder. I must look in the supply closet to see if Zoe has left any behind from one of her craft projects. My niece loves glitter. Zoe isn't really my niece, but I don't know what the correct degree of kinship is. I still think of her as my niece.

Once the dishwasher is loaded, I finish cleaning up the table, collecting the salt and pepper shakers, the sugar dispenser, and the Nutella jar. The creamer goes back in the fridge. And the empty Oreos pack in the trash.

"Uh, wait." I pause as I spot the last Oreo abandoned at the bottom of the tube, a sly grin spreading across my face. I snatch it up triumphantly. That sucker must've missed it.

I take a bite, expecting the sweet, familiar taste of the creamy filling. Instead, my mouth is assaulted by the strong, minty flavor of toothpaste. My eyes water as I force myself not to gag on the vile concoction.

That jackass!

I sputter the crumbs into the bin, coughing madly, and guzzle water straight from the sink to rinse the aftertaste of chocolate and Colgate.

"Something went down the wrong pipe again, Thompson?" A chuckle behind me makes me spin around, my entire face red with both embarrassment and the aftermath of my half-choking fit.

Tristan leans against the door frame, a self-satisfied smirk plastered on his face that would make even a saint want to punch it. It's infuriating how handsome he looks even when he's being a complete and utter bastard. "No." I flash him a mock-sweet smile, hoping there's no black cookie stuck between my teeth. "Just sampling the latest minty Oreo fusion. You should try it; it's... refreshing."

He pushes off from the doorway and strolls over, his blue eyes alight with wickedness. "Glad to hear you're refreshed."

"*So* refreshed."

If he comes a step closer, I'm going to lose my *cool* and unravel like a ball of yarn—or spray him with the sink hose. That would actually be a great idea. I stare at the tube just out of my reach, wondering how fast I can grab it.

Tristan follows my gaze and shakes his head. "Nuh-uh, Thompson." He maneuvers himself between me and the sink.

And why do I feel like my spinal cord has suddenly turned to ice? Or molten lava? I'm not sure if I'm feeling hot or cold. My temperature regulators must be malfunctioning.

Tristan is close now, close enough for me to notice the faint stubble on his jaw and a stray smudge of Nutella at the corner of his mouth. An unbidden thought crosses my mind about how it'd feel to wipe it away with my finger or to lick it off...

"What are you thinking, Thompson?" he drawls.

My eyes snap back to his, guilt flushing my cheeks. "How to put you in your place, *Montgomery*."

He raises an eyebrow, his lips twitching, as if fighting a smile. "And where exactly is my place?" There's a challenge in his voice, wrapped in that velvet tone that makes my stomach do somersaults.

"Far away from here, preferably. In a pit underground with your little demon friends," I retort, trying to maintain a shred of composure despite the heat crawling up my neck.

Unfazed, Tristan reaches behind me for the coffee pot, effectively caging me between the kitchen counter and his hard body, with which I experienced more contact today than in the fifteen years we've known each other.

Still unhurriedly, he reaches for a mug on the shelf above my head and pours himself a coffee with all the calm of a vampire swirling a chalice of fresh blood.

I finally regain some presence of spirit and push him away, beelining for the door. "Wash that mug after you're done."

I turn back as I reach the threshold, only to find him leisurely sipping his coffee while leaning against the counter. He lifts the mug to me in a mock toast. "Sure thing, Thompson, what do you take me for? A savage?"

He's worse than a savage. Tristan Montgomery is a Viking king come to pillage my home, defile my peace, and ruin my holiday cheer.

10

TRISTAN

The cool marble presses into my back as I lean against the counter, a little dazed. The kitchen door swings shut behind Nina.

But even now that she's gone, my mind spins out of control. Every nerve ending under my skin still humming from the feel of her body pressed against mine. What am I doing? I'm an idiot, an idiot playing with fire.

Seeing Nina Thompson naked has scrambled my brain. The way I cornered her just now, my hands on either side of her hips, it's unacceptable. She's Dylan's little sister. Off limits. Untouchable. Always has been.

So why can't I stop staring at the loose strands of hair framing her face? Why does my chest tighten every time she looks at me?

I press my lips together and push away from the counter. This can't happen again. No more pranks, no more provocations. I'll avoid her for the rest of my time here if I have to. My new motto is: do not engage. I only have to survive the holidays, then I can go back to pretending she doesn't exist.

Easier said than done. My traitorous mind is not ready to let go of the memory of how she felt trapped between my body and the counter, the warmth of her skin seeping through my T-shirt, her breath catching as I leaned in close. The way her eyes darkened, lips parting in invitation—

"Enough." I slam my fist on the counter, gritting my teeth. She's not for me. I have to remember that.

When I head into the living room, the entire Thompson family is already there, opening dusty boxes they must've just retrieved from the attic. Right. I should've remembered from my other Christmases with them that they always decorate the tree together. But it's been a few years since the last time I was here for the holidays. Still, my memory is fresh enough to know there's no escaping the tradition. I'm trapped in a room with Nina once again. At least we're not alone.

I'll just keep as far away from her as possible. Or as far as two people working on the same—albeit giant—fir tree can be. I position myself opposite her. From her corner, Nina alternates between openly glaring at me or blatantly ignoring me.

At least that's the act she's putting on. But I also catch her sneaking glances at me when she thinks I'm not looking. And I can't help but notice the blush that stains her cheeks when she realizes I *am* looking in fact. *Interesting.*

No, it's not interesting. It isn't anything.

Because Nina Thompson is off limits. Her brother has hated every single one of her ex-boyfriends, punched at least two—they deserved it, and he's not going to make an exception for me.

With that reminder fresh in my head, I busy myself hanging colorful, uncoordinated ornaments on the higher branches, trying to ignore Nina's presence on the opposite side of the tree. But it's impossible. I can sense her gaze on me like a physical touch, my skin tingling with awareness. My brain tracks her every movement, tuned like a radar with an enemy ship—or, more worryingly, a moth drawn irresistibly to the glow of a warm, flickering flame. But I'm smarter than that. I don't wish to get burned.

Nina is the shortest person in the house, but she still insists on doing the top of the Christmas tree, dragging an old, rickety ladder to her side on which she balances precariously.

She's fixing the lights on the taller branches when Dylan bumps her ladder, sending Nina tumbling into the tree with an "oof!" I am at her side in an instant.

"You okay?" I grasp her waist to steady her, concern overriding my good intentions to stay away.

She blinks up at me, tinsel tangled in her hair, eyes wide. "Yeah, I'm fine."

I realize I am still holding her and settle her on her feet, jerking my hands back as soon as she's stable. Clearing my throat, I take a deliberate step backward. "Good. Just... be more careful."

Nina arches a brow. "What's wrong, Tristan? You prefer your victims fresh before you torture them?"

"You're not my—" I bite off the rest of the protest, refusing to rise to her bait. I've sworn no more responding to provocations—I just have to add no more rushing in for chivalrous rescues and I should be fine.

"It's okay." She pats my arm in a patronizing way. "I won't tell anyone your dark little secret."

What is she talking about? Does she know? She can't know.

I scowl at her. "The only thing I care about is making sure you don't ruin the tree with your clumsiness."

"Sure, bull in a China shop, elephant near a Christmas tree... same thing, right?"

I'm about to snap again that last night's comment wasn't about her when she almost unconsciously fluffs her hair to make sure her ears are covered. Has Nina always been so self-conscious about them? Is that why she hated me calling her Gremlin so much? Did she think the pet name was a jab at her jug ears?

Horror dawns on me. Oh, fuck! I've been a total jerk for years. No wonder she hates my guts. I always called her Gremlin affectionately, because she was so small and cuddly and, well, yes, prone to mischief. But I never meant to offend her.

At the shock on my face, her eyes narrow, and she hisses, "At least try to hide the disgust, Montgomery."

Again, not what I was thinking, but maybe it's better to put up more barriers between us. It'll be easier if she assumes the worst about me.

I take a step back. "Just try to keep upright this time."

I don't correct her assumptions and retreat to my section of the tree, hating myself a little.

Nina huffs and turns away as well, adding more distance between us, her shoulders tense. I watch her go, lost in my own thoughts. How have I never noticed how sensitive she is about her ears? They're not even that big. I must've been a real asshole when I was a teenager.

I sneak a glance at her as she finishes untangling the lights from their clew. Her expression is a mask of indifference, but her back is still stiff. As if sensing my gaze, she stares up at me, and if looks could kill... I'd be six feet under right about now. Her eyes are like two icy daggers that pierce through my soul. I try to look away, but I can't. I'm mesmerized by their fury. And then, in a flash, the frosty rage is gone. Replaced by a flicker of something else. Hurt?

Now I hate myself more than just a little.

Regret washes over me in chilly waves. I'm such an idiot. I never meant to hurt Nina. I always thought our bickering was a silly game. But now I realize that it's been anything but that for her.

I've been cruel, and I've made her feel like she isn't perfect just the way she is.

I watch her fixedly, my mind racing. And then, as fast as the hurt appeared, it's gone. Her eyes go dull again, and she turns back to the tree, untangling the lights with forced nonchalance.

She aggressively ignores me until the tree is nearly done—an explosion of colors and mix-matched decorations that make it look like an elf high on Christmas spirit vomited all his joy on top of it. Nina stands triumphantly on her tiptoes, balancing on the highest step of the ladder. Almost as if she was daring me to reprimand her, to tell her to be more careful as she applies the finishing touches to the tree top. I should scowl, but I can't help staring like a fool, admiring the way the holiday lights illuminate her rosy cheeks while her green eyes sparkle with determination. She seems so innocent at this moment that I almost forget about how merciless her retaliations can be.

I'm almost scared to find out what she has in store next. But I'm pretty sure that between the toothpaste Oreo and the elephant comment I let slide uncorrected, she's going to go for the throat next time. I'll just have to be the bigger person for once and not react.

She catches me staring again and steps down from the ladder with unnecessary acrobatics, again as if she was daring me to tell her off.

Nina stares at me challengingly for a heartbeat, but when I don't say anything, she bends over an empty box of decorations, sticking her pert butt in the air while she rummages inside. I should look away.

For the life of me, I can't.

When she finally straightens up, I let out a breath. Just when I think my suffering is over, she turns my way with a sly glint in her eyes that belies the innocent smile on her lips. I narrow my gaze suspiciously. What is she up to now?

She brushes past me and I relax slightly, thinking I'm in the clear. But then she whirls around at the last second, yelling, "Boo!"

A puff of pink glitter explodes in my face. I sneeze violently, stumbling back in surprise. My elbow knocks into something and a loud crash echoes through the living room.

Blinking the glitter from my eyes, I stare at the shattered remains of one of Mrs. Thompson's antique vases scattered across the floor—the white of the porcelain stark against the dark hardwood. The entire family gapes in shocked silence.

"Nina!" Mrs. Thompson scolds. "Look what you've done!"

"Me?" Nina's mouth falls open in outrage. "I didn't break it, he did! You can't blame me for this."

Mrs. Thompson crosses her arms. "You scared him half to death. What did you expect to happen?"

"It's not my fault if he startles easily," Nina huffs.

"That was your grandmother's vase."

"I know, I didn't break it on purpose. Don't make me responsible for his clumsiness." She points a finger at me.

"You're still accountable for your inhospitality and your childish pranks," Mrs. Thompson retorts with a stern look that has even me straightening my posture out of respect. "This is not the spirit of Christmas."

As their argument escalates, I rub the lingering glitter from my eyes. Leave it to Nina to literally blow up in my face and somehow make it my fault. I suspected she had something planned, yet here I am, still caught unaware—dazzled and disoriented once again.

But as I watch her cheeks flush with indignation, blonde hair falling in fiery waves around her face, I can't help but feel a twisted admiration.

Mrs. Thompson throws her hands up in exasperation. "I can't believe you, Nina. That vase was a family heirloom!"

"Again, not my fault it broke."

I bite back a smirk, but Mrs. Thompson is far from amused. "That's enough. Apologize to Tristan right now."

Nina's green eyes flash with defiance. "Apologize? For what? It's not like I pushed him into the table!" She turns to me, hands on her hips. "Well? Aren't you going to say something? Or are you just going to stand there and let them gang up on me as usual?"

I raise my hands in surrender, knowing better than to get in the middle of a Thompson family showdown. "Hey, I'm just an innocent bystander here. You're the one who assaulted me with a glitter bomb."

"Assaulted?" Nina scoffs. "Oh, don't be so dramatic. It was a harmless prank, and you know it."

Me not admitting it's my fault she blinded me with craft supplies and made me flounder seems to be the final straw.

"You know what? I'm done," Nina declares, stomping her foot in frustration. "I'm so sick of no one ever being on my side in this family. I'm out of here."

With that, she storms off, her footsteps echoing up the stairs before the slam of her bedroom door punctuates her exit. An awkward silence descends over the room in her wake.

I sigh, running a hand through my hair and sending a shower of glitter to the floor. Maybe I should've stepped in. Said something. This is my fault, too. We've both been caught up in this game of one-upmanship, but she's the one dealing with the fallout today. My thoughts race with conflicting emotions—part of me is relieved she definitely won't want anything to do with me after this. The other part yearns to run after her and kiss the anger and frustration away.

"Dylan," Lisa says, turning her attention to her son. "Would you mind helping me clean up?"

"I can do it," I offer, swallowing my mixed feelings and focusing on the task at hand.

Lisa hesitates. "Are you sure?"

"Of course." I give her a gentle nod. "This is partly my fault."

Dylan and his dad make themselves scarce, probably dreading being dragged into the family drama among the Thompson women.

"Oh, Tristan, don't blame yourself. This was all Nina."

"Trust me, Lisa. I know what I'm talking about. Please don't be too hard on your daughter."

I quickly collect the shattered pieces of the vase and place them carefully in a trash bag.

Lisa keeps quiet so long as she sweeps the floor that I don't think she's going to answer me until she says, "Sometimes I wonder if I've been too soft with her."

I grab her by the shoulders. "Nina is an amazing young woman." Then, because I can't bear to look Mrs. Thompson in the eyes as I say this, I hug her. "I just bring out the worst in her."

And that's stopping today.

11

NINA

I launch myself head-first onto my bed, burying my face in the pillow to muffle my frustrated scream. Ugh, this day could not turn any worse. Hot tears sting my eyes as I replay the disastrous prank over and over in my mind. I can't stop crying.

The thing I hate the most is that I let him get to me. In my head, under my skin. And now my family hates me. He can call me Gremlin or Dumbo or put toothpaste in my cookies and he's still everybody's darling. But then I try to exact revenge and suddenly, I'm Miss Undesirable Number One, even to my mother.

What am I even supposed to do until dinner? Should I skip lunch? Search for my mom to apologize?

I'm not sure she's ready to hear anything from me. What would I even say? *"Hey, Mom, sorry I broke your vase while I glitter-bombed the houseguest."*

How could I have been so stupid?

Determined to wallow in self-pity for the rest of the afternoon, I resolutely skip lunch. Even though my stomach rumbles in protest, there's no way I'm risking running into Mom in the kitchen after our showdown. She can say what she wants, but she's even worse than me at holding a grudge. I must've gotten my stubbornness from someone after all.

But by early afternoon, the hunger pangs become too insistent to ignore. Screw it, I think, creeping downstairs and making a beeline for the basement. Dad always keeps a secret stash of junk food squirreled away down there. He thinks no one knows about it, but please—Dylan and I discovered it ages ago, when we were barely tall enough to reach the top shelf, and have been pilfering chocolate bars and bags of chips since when we were kids.

I'm just ripping open a jumbo bag of Doritos when a metallic clang echoes from the laundry room across the way. I freeze with a Dorito halfway to my mouth. No one ever goes in there except to do laundry. And besides the ancient washer and dryer, it's where Dad keeps all his tools and handyman crap.

Another clatter reaches my ears, followed by a muffled curse. Okay, now I have to go investigate. Abandoning the chips, I arm myself with a broomstick and tiptoe over, peering cautiously around the doorframe. My eyes widen at the sight that greets me.

Tristan is hunched over Dad's worktable, brow furrowed in concentration as he fumbles with something in his hands. Is that...? Holy crap, it's a piece of Mom's shattered vase he's trying to glue back together like some 3D jigsaw puzzle. I blink twice to make sure I'm not hallucinating.

Nope, still there. Tristan Montgomery, Prince of Darkness, Satan's minion, the bane of my existence, is actually attempting to repair the antique vase I smashed to smithereens mere hours ago when I attacked him with glitter. I don't know whether to laugh or pinch myself to check again if I'm dreaming. Since when does Mephisto give a flying fart about anyone besides himself?

As if sensing my flabbergasted stare, his head swivels in my direction. For a suspended heartbeat, we just gape at each other in stilted silence, him looking like a demon straight out of hell ready to damn my soul forever; me, angelic, stunned, and kind of slack-jawed.

His gaze shifts from me to the broom in my hands, and his jaw tenses even more. "The glitter bomb didn't work and now you've come to finish the job with a broomstick?"

Shaking myself out of my daze, I ignore the provocation and step fully into the room, dropping the broom into a corner. "Uh, what are you doing there, Tristan?" I aim for breezy nonchalance, but the question comes out more like a strangled cat.

He shoots me a glare that's part annoyance, part embarrassment—a cocktail of emotions that makes him seem almost human. "What does it look like?" he quips back, his hands stilling for just a moment before resuming their meticulous work.

His glue-stained fingers sort through the shards of porcelain that wait patiently to be reassembled.

"Uh-huh. Playing hero?" I sidle closer, craning my neck to peer at his handiwork. Damn, he's actually made decent headway already. The base of the vase is standing under the overhead spotlight, perfectly rebuilt. "Don't worry, you're everybody's darling already."

Tristan huffs and rolls his eyes, but I catch the way the tips of his ears pinken before he turns away. "Just trying to fix something that shouldn't have been broken," he mutters, clearly referring to more than just the vase.

I cross my arms, leaning against my father's tool panel. Well, well, well. Seems like Tristan Montgomery might have a conscience after all. Will the wonders never cease?

I edge closer to the table, my fingers itching to pick up a shard. Before I can think better of it, the words tumble out of my mouth. "Want some help?"

Tristan's head snaps up, his jaw going taut as his gaze lands on me. Oh gosh, he must really hate me. I fidget under the intensity of his glare, second-guessing my offer. But now that it's out there, my pride won't let me back down. Nina Thompson is no quitter.

Squaring my shoulders, I march over to the table and plop myself down on the stool beside him. I pluck a glittering piece of porcelain from the pile, twirling it between my fingers. "I mean, we broke it together. Seems only fair we fix it together, too."

Tristan stares at me for a long moment, his eyes narrowing as if deciding if he should contradict me. His expression is unreadable, unnerving. Then, with a put-upon sigh, he slides a few shards my way. "Fine. But don't make it worse than it already is."

I scoff, affronted. "Ye of little faith. I'll have you know I'm excellent at puzzles."

"Is that what they're calling vandalism these days?" he mumbles under his breath.

I elbow him in the ribs, earning a satisfying grunt. "Shut up and pass the glue, Montgomery."

As Tristan hands me the bottle of superglue, our fingers brush and a jolt of something zigzags up my arm. His eyes meet mine, and the air between us gets all charged up like right before a summer storm. But I refuse to be the first one fried by lightning, so I quickly grab the glue and start applying a thin line to the edge of a shard. We work in silence for a few minutes, the tension thick enough to slice through with a butter knife.

There's a new tautness in his shoulders that wasn't there when I was observing him unseen from the doorframe. Do I make him nervous? I'm not sure if I should talk or keep quiet. But after a while, I can't bear the pressure of the silence engulfing us anymore.

"You know," I break the quiet, my voice light, teasing, "the way you're holding that piece... it's like you're afraid it's going to leap out of your hand and attack."

He snorts. "Not worried about the porcelain."

"You wouldn't be anxious about innocent little me?" I quip, glancing at the way his fingers are delicately balancing the intricate piece.

Tristan doesn't rise to the bait, instead, he focuses on fitting a tiny shard into place. His technique is admittedly impressive, each move meticulous and sure.

I get kind of hypnotized by how his large hands can handle such tiny pieces with innate precision. Even more distractingly, the sleeves of his sweater are rolled up, showcasing disturbingly sexy forearms.

The unsettling combo of power and grace has me wondering how those hands would feel on my bare skin; if those arms could lift me off the floor as easily as they look capable of.

Until his next words slap me back to the present. "Innocent is the *last* word I'd use to describe you, Nina," he responds, not looking up.

"Oh, really?" I challenge, tilting my head to one side to give him a mock glare. "What would you say is a good descriptor?"

When he doesn't respond, I provoke him. "Right, we all know the terms you prefer to use when it comes to me."

Finally, Tristan glances up, his blue eyes locking with mine. "None of what you're thinking I'm thinking is what I'm actually thinking."

I frown. "Are you trying to sidetrack me with bad sentence structuring?"

He sighs. "Just work, Nina. Or even better, go away."

The way he says Nina, on a long exhale, lands straight at the base of my spine. I decide keeping quiet is the wisest choice and finally hold my tongue. I find a piece he's missing and hand it to him. He takes it with a small nod.

And just like that, we fall into an oddly comfortable rhythm, our heads bent close in concentration. It's almost... nice. Who would've thought Tristan and I could actually work together without killing each other?

As the minutes tick by, the tension that always seems to crackle between us slowly dissipates, replaced by a tentative camaraderie. I sneak glances at him from the corner of my eye, marveling at the way his brow furrows when he's deep in thought and how his long fingers deftly maneuver the delicate shards.

"I think this piece goes here," I murmur, holding up another particularly tricky fragment. Tristan leans in to inspect it, his shoulder brushing against mine. I inhale sharply, caught off guard by his proximity, by the clean, spicy scent of his cologne.

"Good eye," he concedes, taking the piece from my hand and fitting it into place. Our fingers touch briefly, sending another jolt of electricity up my arm. I yank my arm back as if scalded, my heart doing a little flip in my chest.

Get a grip, Nina. It's just Tristan. Annoying, infuriating, unfairly attractive Tristan.

We keep at our task for a few more silent minutes, the only sounds the clink of ceramic and the occasional murmured direction. Finally, Tristan sets down the last piece with a dramatic flair. "There. Good as new."

I lean back to admire our handiwork. The vase looks almost perfect, the cracks are barely visible. "Not bad, Montgomery. Who knew you had a hidden talent for arts and crafts?"

His gaze sweeps upward in exasperation, yet his posture loosens. "I'm a man of many talents."

"Mm, like being a pain in my ass?"

"Among other things." He stares at me sideways, tilting his head. My cheeks heat in response to the scrutiny.

Hopping off the stool, I perch on the edge of the worktable, needing some distance. I study him, chewing on my bottom lip. "Why did you do this, really?"

Tristan sighs, shaking his head. For a second, I think he's going to ignore me and brush off the question like he always does. But then he meets my gaze, his blue eyes startlingly earnest. "I'm not the monster you believe me to be."

I blink, taken aback by his unexpected vulnerability. Part of me wants to give him the benefit of the doubt. Trust the sincerity I see in his eyes. But the other part, the part that's been burned before, holds back.

"They say the devil's biggest trick is to convince us he doesn't exist," I say softly, holding his stare. "Is that what you're doing, Tristan? Trying to trick me?"

Tristan surprises me by stepping forward and placing himself between my legs. My thoughts scatter as he reaches out, his fingers grazing my cheek as he tucks a strand of hair behind my ear. Instinctively, I jerk back, my hand flying up to cover my ear, to conceal the flaw that has always been the source of my insecurities. That he's mocked countless times.

"Don't," he commands, his voice low and firm. He catches my wrist, pulling my hand away. "Your ears are perfect, Nina."

I scoff, incredulous. "Are you kidding me? You're the one who made fun of them in the first place!"

"I was a stupid kid," he says, his thumb brushing over the shell of my ear. "I didn't know any better."

I want to pull away, to put some distance between us, but I'm frozen, trapped by the unyielding focus in his eyes. "And now? What's your excuse now?"

"Now?" He leans in, his breath warm against my skin. "Now, I think they're adorable. They're part of what makes you... you."

My heart stutters in my chest, a traitorous flutter of hope and longing. But I push that feeling down, shove it into the same box where I keep all the other things I don't know what to do with— like my inexplicable attraction to this infuriating man.

I need to regain control, to remind myself who he is, who we are. "I thought you said you weren't trying to trick me," I manage, my voice shakier than I'd like.

His eyes search mine, a flicker of something raw and real in their depths. "I'm not. For once in my life, Nina, I'm being completely honest with you."

There's a sincerity in his voice that rattles my defenses.

I'm not sure if I want to laugh in his face or cry or kiss him silly. My mind's a whirlwind of confusion. "W-what are you saying?" My words come out labored. We're standing too close. His proximity is disarming in a way that it's never been before.

Tristan's fingers softly graze my jawline, stirring sensations that ought to be forbidden. "What I'm saying is…" He pauses, and his silence is thick with the weight of all that's gone unsaid over the years. His thumb reaches the edge of my mouth and stops. His gaze drops to my slightly parted lips to then collide with me again, tortured.

He leans closer still and my lips part further in anticipation, but then Tristan takes a step back and shakes his head.

"Just stay out of my way, Nina."

After that ultimate rejection, he turns and leaves. I'm half tempted to grab the vase we just reconstructed and throw it at his head.

I can't believe I almost let Tristan Montgomery kiss me. Worse even, I *wanted* him to kiss me. He's the one who put a stop to it.

I brace my arms on the table for support, my heart still pounding like a jackhammer. I should be angry—I *am* angry, furious—but there's this annoying little twinge of disappointment that won't go away.

I stare at the spot where Tristan stood moments ago, my mind reeling. His words, his touch, the way he looked at me… it's all too much to process. I want to scream, to break something, to demand answers. But I'm paralyzed, caught in a web of emotions I can't sort.

But one thing is certain, from now on, I won't let my guard down around him. Not even for a second. He'll just use any vulnerability he can find to destroy me.

My stomach growls, reminding me of the reason I came down here in the first place. I hop off the worktable, and my leggings get caught on an old rusty nail, ripping in the back.

Just perfect.

Cursing under my breath, I stomp into the other room and eat out my feelings, severely depleting Dad's secret stash.

12

TRISTAN

I sprint up the stairs from the basement as if fleeing the scene of a crime and burst into my room, slamming the door behind me. It clicks and swings back open.

"Oh, you've got to be kidding me," I growl, shoving it closed again. Same thing—the latch refuses to catch. I kick the door in frustration, but it just bounces right back, mocking me.

Taking a deep breath, I try a gentler approach, slowly easing the latch into position until I hear a satisfying click. Finally.

I slump back against the wooden panels and run a hand through my hair. What the hell is wrong with me? What was that in the basement? I was this close to kissing the living hell out of her. Every time I'm alone with Nina for more than thirty seconds, I end up ravishing her like some kind of crazed animal. First pinning her against the kitchen counter, then her father's worktable...

The memory has the opposite effect of cooling me down. I curse under my breath. This is my best friend's little sister, for fuck's sake. I need to get a grip.

But it's like there's some invisible magnet drawing me to her, short-circuiting my brain until all I can think about is biting that petulant mouth and—

No. I shake my head firmly. This has to stop. The only solution is to make sure I'm never alone with her again. I'll stick to Dylan like a shadow from now on. Can't risk any more... slip-ups.

I scrub a hand down my face and sigh. When did my life get so complicated? Time was, Nina Thompson was just a gangly kid with a sharp tongue and an annoying tendency to pester me. Now she's all grown up and sexier than hell—and apparently still determined to torment me at every turn.

Pushing off the door, I start pacing the room, trying to walk off my pent-up energy. Nina's pouty lips and flashing green eyes keep floating through my mind unbidden. I feel like a kid with his first crush and a dirty old man, all at the same time.

"Get it together, Montgomery," I mutter. I'm acting worse than a hormonal teenager instead of the thirty-three-year-old man I am.

But something about Nina just brings out my most primal instincts—an irresistible urge to touch, to taste, to claim. It's downright Neanderthal of me. She'd probably knee me in the groin if she knew the filthy thoughts running through my head right now. Even if the way she parted her lips for me in the basement might suggest otherwise.

Would she have let me kiss her?

It. Doesn't. Matter. Because I'm not going to kiss her. Period.

I collapse on the bed and let out a long groan of frustration. It's only another two days before Christmas, I can make it until then without doing something monumentally stupid. And after, I should leave early with an excuse. A work emergency or something. Anything to escape this constant, all-consuming tug of war between wanting her and knowing I absolutely shouldn't.

My eyelids droop heavily as I stretch out on the mattress. Bone-deep exhaustion seeps through me. The sleepless night is catching up with me all at once. Nina's fault again, of course. That infernal prank with the alarm clocks blaring at unholy hours. The woman's diabolical...

I yawn as coherent thoughts slip away and sleep drags me under. The bed is soft, the pillow cool against my cheek. I'll deal with Nina later...

Bang!

I jolt awake, ears ringing. What the hell? Blinking blearily, I try to get my bearings. Bed, pillow, fading daylight through the window. I'm in the guest room at Dylan's. And that noise—that loud bang...

Definitely a door slamming. And I know exactly which door, and who's behind it. Nina. Waking me on purpose, no doubt, in petty retaliation for... something. Breathing. Existing.

Well, two can play that game. Irritation surges through me, shoving back the cobwebs of sleep. I'm on my feet and out the door before reason can kick in.

I don't bother knocking, just barge right into her room, ready to give her a piece of my mind. Let her see how she likes rude awakenings and invaded privacy and—

The angry tirade dies on my tongue as I pull up short, blinking stupidly. Whatever I was expecting, it wasn't this.

Nina stands frozen by her dresser, eyes wide and startled. She's wearing that oversized sweater from earlier, all soft and cuddly looking. And on her feet, those ridiculous Grinch slippers. But below the hem of the sweater... miles of bare legs.

Holy shit. My brain short-circuits, anger momentarily forgotten as I gawk at those long, toned limbs on display. The sweater hits her upper mid-thigh, and I can't tell if she's even wearing underwear. The thought sends all my blood rushing south.

"Tristan?" Her startled query snaps me out of my daze. "What are you doing here?"

I drag my eyes up to her face, trying to remember how to form words. What am I doing here? Good fucking question.

"I... you woke me," I manage lamely. "With the door. Slamming."

She lifts an eyebrow, unimpressed. "And you decided to, what, storm into my room and give me a good spanking?"

Those are not words she should utter in my presence. Now the idea of how easy it would be to do just that—pull her across my knees and lift up that sweater to reveal her pantless ass—is etched into my brain. So are other wild fantasies that would make Christian Gray look like a domesticated teddy bear.

At my lack of answer, her arms cross over her chest, one slipper-clad foot tapping the floor. The movement draws my attention back to her bare legs. Oh, man.

I swallow hard, scrambling for coherent thoughts. This was a bad idea. I should leave before I do something reckless. Like cross the room and pin her against that dresser. I mean, I already have kitchen counter and basement worktable in my repertoire, what's a little bedroom dresser addition?

I take a step back, intent on retreating while I still can. But then Nina's gaze dips to my mouth, her teeth sinking into her plump lower lip. And just like that, all rational thoughts evaporate.

Sleep deprivation. That's what this is. Sleep deprivation and forced proximity and the maddening effect this woman has always had on me. A perfect storm of bad influences eroding my self-control. I'm drunk on exhaustion and stupidity and want—a want so visceral it scares me. But suddenly, I know exactly what I'm doing in her room and I go to her, determined to see my madness through.

13

NINA

Forty minutes earlier

Humiliation, thy name is Nina Thompson. I scarf down the last of the Doritos, licking the cheese dust off my fingers. But even that fails to console my wounded pride after Tristan's latest rejection. My stomach grumbles, unsatisfied.

I get on tiptoe to check what else Dad has stashed aside and spot, tucked behind the jumbo box of Fruit Loops, his contraband chocolate peanut caramel bars. Bingo. I devour two in rapid succession, letting the gooey sweetness momentarily chase away the bitter aftertaste of Tristan's snub.

When the sugar high fades, I'm left with ripped pants, a belly full of junk, and the urge to hide in this basement forever. Mom's idea to banish me was actually a small mercy. At this point, I'm too ashamed to face half the people in this house. Make it *all* the people in the house except for myself. Tristan is Tristan. My parents are disappointed with me because of the vase. And I don't suppose Dylan would be happy if he knew the naughty fantasies I've been harboring about his best friend. Or that we almost kissed.

But I can't stay here all afternoon. The book I was reading is upstairs and the only things down here are an old, sagging couch and Dylan's gaming console. Time to sneak back to my room.

I tiptoe up the stairs, ears straining for any sign of human activity. The house is quieter than one of Dad's mandatory fishing trips. At the top of the basement stairs, I dart across the hall and up the second flight of stairs to the first floor, ready to hole back up in my room until I'll eventually have to show my face for dinner and repent. I almost half expect to find a septa crawling in the hallway while ringing a bell to the chant of, "Shame, shame..."

I'm about to reach the relative safety of my room, when I freeze just outside my door, pulse drumming in my ears. Tristan's door stands ajar, an open invitation. It must be the faulty hinge—that door always swings open on its own. From here, I can only see his feet—shoes still on—at the edge of the bed. The view mocks me, daring me to sneak one more peek at the slumbering devil.

I hover indecisively, tugged by temptation, knowing I should bolt to the security of my room. But my feet betray me, inching closer to his lair. One harmless little glance can't hurt, right?

My feet keep moving of their own accord, and I find myself poised at Tristan's threshold. The sight of him, dark lashes sealed in sleep, full lips parted, hair falling over his forehead, skewers my insides like a bolt of lightning. I drink him in, unable to tear my eyes away. He looks utterly peaceful, almost innocent. More fallen angel than ousted devil.

I inch closer, captivated by the rise and fall of his chest. In sleep, the ever-present smirk is wiped from his face, replaced by a boyish vulnerability that makes my treacherous heart flutter. Damn him. Even in an unconscious state, Tristan has me under his spell.

A sigh escapes his lips and I freeze, terrified he'll wake and catch me creeping. But he merely shifts, his sweater riding higher over his sculpted stomach, and settles back into dreaming. My eyes linger where they shouldn't, tracing the contours of his body and that sliver of exposed skin like I have any right to commit them to memory.

And that's when it hits me—the sheer absurdity of the situation. Here I am, gawking at my nemesis while he's blissfully unaware, half an hour after swearing off him for good. Pathetic. The humiliation from the basement comes rushing back in technicolor—Tristan's rejection. *"Just stay out of my way, Nina."*

That's exactly what I should do. White-hot anger surges through my veins, momentarily eclipsing my fascination. How dare he make me feel this way, even now? I clench my fists, overcome by the petty urge to shatter his peaceful rest.

I back away from the door, mind whirring with the perfect plan for vengeance. It's juvenile, sure, but I'm past the point of caring. Tristan brought this on himself.

With a final scowl in his direction, I whirl around and stomp into my room with all the grace of a crazed elephant—aha, he wanted an elephant, I'll give him one.

Bang!

The door slams behind me with a satisfying crash, rattling the very walls with my fury. Take that, you insufferable man-devil.

I can only imagine the rude awakening he's getting right now, bolting upright in bed with his dark hair deliciously rumpled and eyes wide with confusion. The mental image brings a smirk of savage satisfaction to my face. Immature? Absolutely. But revenge is sweet.

I've just managed to shimmy out of my torn leggings and slip on my fuzzy green slippers when my bedroom door suddenly flies open with a second bang. I turn around, my mouth falling open as I discover Tristan framed in the doorway like some dark avenging angel. He steps inside and shuts the door firmly behind him. Those piercing blue eyes narrowed on me.

"Tristan?" I squeak, trying to play it cool despite the frantic pounding of my pulse. "What are you doing here?"

He runs a hand through his sleep-tousled hair, looking momentarily taken aback by the question. As if he's not sure himself. "I... you woke me. With the door. Slamming."

Tristan's gaze rakes over me, lingering on my bare legs before snapping back to my face. A muscle ticks in his jaw, and I swear the temperature in the room ratchets up a few degrees.

I arch an eyebrow, feigning nonchalance even as my stomach does cartwheels under his penetrating stare. "And you decided to, what, storm into my room and give me a good spanking?"

The words slip out before I can stop them, whipping across the space between us like a challenge. What is wrong with me? I mentally face-palm, bracing for Tristan's scathing comeback.

But he just stands there, an odd expression flickering across his chiseled features. Is that... uncertainty? From the unflappable Tristan Montgomery?

No, I must be imagining things. This is the man who takes perverse pleasure in tormenting me at every turn. The one who callously shattered my dignity less than an hour ago in the basement.

I straighten my spine, determined not to let him see how much he affects me. How the mere sight of him sets my blood thrumming and my knees wobbling. I'll be damned if I give him the satisfaction.

I tap my foot and he looks at it, then back at my legs.

What is that look in his eyes? It's intense, almost... hungry. Like a predator sizing up its prey. My skin prickles with awareness, and I'm suddenly acutely aware of my state of undress. Did I shave this morning in the shower? Please tell me I shaved.

Get a grip, Nina. This is Tristan we're talking about. The bane of your existence. The man who seems to delight in pushing your buttons at every opportunity.

But then why is he looking at me like that, his blue eyes darkening with some unreadable emotion? Why isn't he firing back with a witty retort or mocking jab?

The distance between us grows, filled with an undefinable strain that words can't capture. My heart is a wild thing in my chest as all the hair on my body—hopefully none on my legs—stands to attention.

Finally, Tristan backtracks. It looks like he's decided to stand down for once. And since he's about to leave, I let my gaze drop to his mouth. To those full, luscious lips that were about to kiss me and that he denied me.

He seems to notice because the retreat stops.

Instead of going away, Tristan takes a step forward, then another, his gaze never leaving mine. A new determination is etched on his beautiful face. I instinctively back up until the solid press of the wall behind me stops me. I'm trapped.

He looms over me, close enough that I can feel the heat radiating off his body. Smell the intoxicating scent of him—warm male and crisp cotton tinged with the barest hint of spice.

Time seems to stall as he braces a hand against the wall beside my head, caging me in. His other hand comes to rest on my hip, his touch searing even through the thick fabric of my sweater.

I stare up at him with a mix of awe and trepidation. Speckles of glitter are still trapped in his eyelashes and a few dust his cheeks. It should be ridiculous, but it's mesmerizing instead.

"I'm going to kiss you, Nina," he rasps, his voice low and rough like sandpaper. "If you don't want me to, say so now."

My mind goes blank, all sentient thoughts evaporating under

the fiery determination in his stare. I know I should protest, push him away, tell him exactly where he can stick his kiss...

But I can't seem to form the words. Or do anything but gaze up at him, my lips parting on a shaky exhale.

Tristan's eyes flare with triumph, with a heat that sets my blood on fire. He dips his head, his mouth hovering a hairsbreadth from mine.

"Last chance, sweetheart," he murmurs, his breath fanning across my lips. A final, playful warning.

We stare at each other in a sort of standoff. I should say something. Laugh in his face, push him away. Instead, I'm enthralled in his blue glaciers and can only swallow and wet my lips as an invisible pressure threatens to make me implode.

The move doesn't escape Tristan. His gaze drops to my mouth only to snap back to me, darker now. Almost feral. He tilts his head in a final, silent question, and when I still say nothing, he pulls me into him with a force contrasting the gentle way his lips press on mine.

Oh gosh, his mouth feels as damning as it looks. Soft and firm all at once. My pulse skyrockets while small explosions go off in my belly. And he hasn't even started to really kiss me yet. He's just toying with me.

Just as his mouth presses more insistently on mine, demanding access, there's a knock on my door and my brother's voice filters through. "Nina, you in there?"

My heart can't take it. Between the clandestine kiss, and my brother now at the door ready to discover us, I dissolve into a cloud of panic.

14

TRISTAN

The sound of Dylan knocking on the door jolts through me like a live wire. I pull away from Nina's intoxicating kiss—not sure if I've been saved or doomed by the interruption. My entire body is buzzing as I take in her emerald eyes that have never looked bigger and her pouty lips, swollen and still parted for me. Damn, she looks like my personal heaven and hell rolled into one.

She isn't moving or saying anything, she's just staring at me. And it's like looking into a green forest, a shocked, enthralling woodland.

Dylan knocks again, impatient. When Nina still doesn't move, I lean in, my lips grazing the shell of her ear.

"Tell him you need a minute," I whisper. Goosebumps prickle across her skin. She nods, dazed, eyes unwaveringly locked on mine.

"Just a second!" she calls, her voice hitching. I glance around the room, searching for a place to hide. There's no way I'm crawling out the window like some pimply teenager. Especially not when it's in the low twenties outside.

"Is there somewhere to hide?" I ask. Nina's gaze darts to the bed. I narrow my eyes. "I'm not hiding under your bed," I hiss.

She huffs and shoves me toward the walk-in closet instead. I stumble inside, nearly tripping over a pile of shoes before Nina slams the door in my face.

Next, I hear her yank open the bedroom door. I can almost picture Dylan standing on the other side, arms crossed impatiently.

"Hello, brother," she says, overly bright. I wince. Could she be any more obvious? This is going to hell fast. I'm a dead man. Dylan will discover me and mount my head on his bedroom wall.

Irrationally—Dylan can't see me either way—I press my back against the back of the closet, the ridges of Nina's shoe rack digging into my spine. Holding my breath, I strain to hear their voices through the door.

"Hello, *sister*," Dylan replies, drawing out the words. He's definitely suspicious. I picture his eyebrows shooting up, the way they always do when he's onto something. "Why aren't you wearing pants?"

Yeah, great question, buddy. I'm curious to hear the answer myself.

"Oh, I ripped them." Nina's voice is an octave too high. "In the basement. I was just changing."

Silence. I can practically hear the gears turning in Dylan's head.

"The basement?" Dylan asks slowly. "Funny, that's why I came up. Mom found the vase you glued back together. She's not mad anymore. You should go down and apologize to her while she's mollified."

My nose itches, and I fight the urge to sneeze. Getting busted because of dusty cashmere would be a new low, even for me.

"Right. Yes. I'll go now." Nina's voice wobbles.

I don't even mind that she hasn't given me credit for helping with the vase. Dylan can't know. No one can know. Especially not after that half-kiss that I'm dying and dreading to finish.

"Are you sure you're alright?" Dylan asks. I can practically see the frown on his face.

"Yeah, sure, I'm golden. Nothing is going on."

Gosh, Nina, why don't you tell him you have his best friend stashed in your closet? You'd sound less guilty. But as long as Dylan doesn't open this door, we're fine. I've never been claustrophobic, but I'm starting to feel the walls inch closer. The air turns stale in my lungs. It's okay. I can handle five more minutes in my best friend's sister's closet.

"I'll go apologize to Mom, at once," Nina says, still sounding agitated.

"Wait." What now? "Shouldn't you wear pants first?"

"Pants, sure." Nina lets out a hysterical chuckle. "I'll just grab a pair *from my closet*." She practically screams those last words.

"Right." Dylan clears his throat. He must be super weirded-out.

That's my clue to slink further into the shadows. I flatten myself against the darkest corner of the closet where I shouldn't be visible even with the door open.

As if on cue, the door flies open, and Nina slips inside. In the dim light, her eyes shine like emeralds, wide and luminous. She glowers at me, I smirk.

Still staring daggers at me, she steps closer, reaching for the shelf above my head. Her soft, fuzzy sweater rides up, revealing even more smooth skin on her toned legs. I swallow hard.

Nina rises on tiptoe, her body grazing mine. The heat of her seeps through my sweater, igniting a fire in my veins. She stretches higher, and her chest brushes against me. I clench my jaw, fighting the urge to haul her against me and pick up where we left off.

Focus, Montgomery. Your best friend is standing just outside that door and would beat you into a pulp if he found you in his sister's room looking ready to devour her like a wolf eyeing a particularly juicy lamb chop.

But as Nina fumbles for her pants, her breath warm on my neck, I can't help myself. I flatten my palm against the small of her back, steadying her. She tenses, her eyes snapping to mine.

I let my hand wander up her spine, relishing the shiver that runs through her. I go higher, skimming her nape, then softly thread my fingers through her hair. Goosebumps erupt on her skin.

Nina parts her lips, a protest forming. I silence her with a look, my hand sliding down, down, until I'm moving over the curve of her ass and lower still. My fingertips graze the inside of her thigh.

She goes very still, eyes wide and questioning. I drink it in, tracing lazy circles on her soft skin. Moving higher, slowly, an inch at a time. Her breath hitches.

"Hey, Nina?" Dylan's voice shatters the moment. "Have you seen Tristan?"

Nina jolts back, snatching her pants from the shelf. "What? No! Why would I have seen Tristan?"

She stumbles out of the closet, leaving the door ajar. I press myself into the rack, holding my breath.

"I've been looking for him, but he's not in his room and I can't find him anywhere."

"He's probably off to polish his horns or something." Her laugh is reedy, cracking at the edges.

She glares at me from the closet doorway, her mouth pressed into a tight line of disapproval. I can't resist. I blow her a kiss, my smirk widening as her eyes narrow to slits.

"Look, I know you two don't like each other," Dylan says, his voice laced with exasperation. "But could you please stop trying to maim my best friend and just be civil for the rest of the holidays?"

Nina huffs, tearing her gaze from mine to face her brother. "I can't make any promises."

I watch her pull up her pants and something burns in my chest, a new feeling I don't dare name. It's more than just attraction, more than the thrill of the chase. It's something deeper, something that terrifies and exhilarates me in equal measure.

Dylan sighs. "Just... try, okay? For me."

"Fine," Nina grumbles. "But if he starts something, I reserve the right to retaliate."

I bite back a laugh. Oh, I'll start *something*, alright. And her retaliation will be my prize.

"Whatever." Dylan sighs. "If you see him, tell him I'm looking for him."

Dylan's footsteps retreat, the door closing behind him. Nina whirls on me, her eyes flashing. "You," she hisses, stalking toward the closet. "Get out of here before my brother finds you and murders you."

I step out of the shadows, my hands raised in mock surrender. "Eager to get rid of me, Thompson?" I inch closer. "You didn't seem to mind me a minute ago."

She jabs a finger into my chest. "I don't know what game you're playing, but it's not cool."

I catch her wrist, tugging her closer. "Oh, I think it was very *cool*. In fact, I'd say it was downright... electrifying."

Nina gasps, her pulse jumping beneath my fingers. For a moment, we stare at each other, as an unspoken challenge pulses through the stillness.

Then she wrenches her arm free, backing away. "This never happened," she says, her voice shaking. "And it will never happen again."

I watch her go, my Adam's apple bobbing. She's right, of course she is. This should never have happened, it shouldn't happen again. But now that I've had a taste, I'm not sure I could keep away even if I wanted to. So, no, Nina, if only you knew how wrong you are.

A second later, my phone buzzes in my pocket—it's Dylan texting me asking me where the hell I am. Right, I'd better come up with a great excuse for where I've been in the past two hours. But not before I send a little teasing text to my favorite troublemaker.

15

NINA

My phone pings as I'm descending the stairs. I fish it out of my pocket and my heart nearly stops when I see the message:

THE PRINCE OF DARKNESS

If you want to polish my horns later, darling, all you have to do is ask. *smiley devil emoji*

I freeze mid-step, gripping the banister. Memories of the kiss come flooding back—Tristan's strong hands on my waist, his lips firm and insistent against mine, the taste of evil seduction on his breath. It was electric, intoxicating... and over far too soon thanks to my brother's untimely intrusion.

I close my eyes, reliving the way Tristan touched me in the closet next, his fingers trailing fire along my legs. A shiver races down my spine. What is he playing at? Is this just another one of his games, part of his endless mission to get under my skin and toy with my emotions? Kiss me senseless one moment and toss me aside the next?

I inhale deeply, trying to calm my labored breathing. I can't let myself fall for Tristan's charms, no matter how much my traitorous body wants to melt into his touch. He's danger wrapped in a dark-haired, blue-eyed package. My brother's best friend. A notorious heartbreaker.

Steeling my resolve, I right my spine and continue down the stairs, locking my phone without replying. Two can play this game, Montgomery. And I have no intention of losing... even if resisting him may be the greatest challenge of my life.

I find Mom in the kitchen, unloading the dishwasher. "Hey," I say softly, biting my lip. "I'm really sorry about the vase. I didn't mean to—"

She turns, her face softening as she pulls me into a hug. "Oh, honey. It's okay. It was an accident."

Relief washes over me as I sink into her embrace, inhaling the comforting scent of her vanilla perfume. "Thanks, Mom."

"Are you hungry?" she asks, pulling back to study my face. "I can whip up some pancakes or—"

"No, I'm good," I assure her.

"But you skipped lunch."

"I um... found something to eat." I keep vague, not wanting to rat on my dad.

Mom's eyes narrow. "You mean you raided your father's *secret* stash." She makes air quotes over secret.

My mouth dangles open. Mom knows about Dad's clandestine junk food supply?

At my shocked expression, she bursts out laughing. "Oh, baby, nothing goes on in this house that I don't know about."

I can't help it; I flush red from head to toe. I hope there is at least *something* going on in this house that she doesn't know about. Like her daughter canoodling with the evil houseguest.

I force myself to join in her laughter, the tension still taut in my shoulders as I try to push thoughts of the Prince of Confusing Me aside. "Like father, like daughter, I guess."

The back door opens and Tristan himself strolls in, his cheeks flushed from the cold, a dusting of snow in his midnight hair. Heat pools in my core as our eyes meet, invisible wires connecting us.

He smirks, shrugging off his coat. "What's so funny?"

Before I can come up with a snarky retort, Dylan also enters the kitchen, clapping Tristan on the shoulder. "There you are. Was your stroll in the Arctic fun?"

Tristan must've used the excuse of going for a walk to cover his tracks and explain his disappearance. Now, eyes never leaving mine, he says, "Oh, the chill outside has nothing on the heat I've found indoors."

If spines could melt, I'd be an invertebrate by now.

"That's poetic, I guess." Dylan coughs, unsure. To him and Mom, Tristan probably isn't making any sense. "But if you're done channeling your inner Elsa, are you ready to lose at *Call of Duty*, Eleven?"

I roll my eyes at the fact that they still call each other by their college basketball numbers.

Tristan tears his gaze away from mine, grinning at my brother. "In your dreams, Thirty-three."

As they head down to the basement, their good-natured ribbing fading away, I release a shaky breath. Being in the same room as Tristan is dangerous, every single one of my senses is attuned to his presence.

Even if I've been pardoned and my exile revoked, I retreat to my bedroom, needing space to clear my head. Slumping onto my bed, I grab my phone and shoot a group text to my best friends.

NINA

The Prince of Darkness kissed me.

face screaming in fear emoji

kiss mark emoji

Their responses come in a vortex of multiple pings, a mix of shock, awe, and concern. But before I can even compose a reply, my phone rings with a three-way video call. I pick up, glad to hear their voices.

"Spill. Everything. Now," Hunter demands before I've had time to say hello.

I launch into the whole sordid tale—Tristan's sudden appearance, the escalating pranks, the charged moment in the basement, the toe-curling semi-kiss, and the groping in the closet. "If Dylan hadn't interrupted..." I trail off, my cheeks burning.

"Whoa," Rowena breathes. "That's... intense."

"Too intense," Hunter warns. "Sweetie, be careful. Tristan Montgomery has left a trail of broken hearts from New York to Hawaii. I don't want you to be his next conquest."

I sigh, knowing she's right. "I know, I know. It's just... when he touches me, I forget how to think straight."

"So you don't hate him anymore?" Rowena asks. "After all those years of him calling you Gremlin."

I realize one thing now that she mentions it. "He hasn't called me Gremlin once since he got here."

Hunter scrunches her face on the screen. "What do you think that means?"

"I have no clue. Should I ask him?"

"Would you trust whatever he said back?"

"I don't knooow," I groan.

"Stay strong," Rowena encourages. "Don't let him get in your head... or your heart."

"Or your bed," Hunter trills.

"Easier said than done," I mutter, glancing at the clock. "I gotta go, dinner's almost ready. Pray for me."

As I end the call with Rowena and Hunter, a smile lingers on my face. No matter what kind of mood I'm in, talking with my best friends always lifts my spirits. They are truly my soul sisters.

I tap my screen and stare at the wallpaper. It's a selfie of us taken almost ten years ago on the night we met. We're all wearing similar pink dresses, standing facing the camera in various states of disarray. Hair wet from the rain, melting makeup running down our cheeks, and in Rowena's case, the aftermath of an allergic reaction still very visible under her bright smile.

My mind wanders back to that fateful Halloween our sophomore year of college. Unlike Tristan and Dylan, who were randomly slapped together in the same dorm room their freshman year, the three of us had to find each other. And find each other we did, in the only twenty-four-hour diner on campus, just after midnight.

As I pushed open the door, eager to escape the beating rain and an even stingier humiliation, a little bell jingled overhead. Glancing around the nearly empty diner, my eyes landed on another girl hunched over a giant milkshake in a corner booth. I did a double-take.

Hunter was wearing an Elle Woods costume, just like me. Pink dress, blonde wig—her, I kept my already natural blonde hair—and a toy chihuahua in her purse. For a second, we gaped at each other, jaws dropping. Then, as if on cue, the door chimed again and Rowena, also dressed as Elle, stepped in. We all stared at each other, bewildered, and then Hunter waved us over.

Introductions were made, and we began chatting like old friends, a little gigglier than was polite. But we didn't care even as the other late-night patrons shot us annoyed looks. I couldn't help but marvel at the serendipity of it all. How three lonely, drenched souls could find such an instant connection.

Now, my gaze drifts to the framed photo of the three of us on my desk. It was taken on graduation day, our faces glowing with pride and possibility. So much has changed since then, but our friendship remains a constant comfort.

I can't help but chuckle as specific details from that first chance meeting flood back. How Hunter dramatically recounted fleeing a house party after a fog machine fiasco, complete with wild hand gestures that nearly knocked over her chocolate milkshake.

"I panicked!" she exclaimed. "One minute I'm shimmying to 'Monster Mash,' the next I'm stumbling into that damn machine. Smoke everywhere! People coughing and running for the exits. I wanted to die of embarrassment right there."

Rowena and I howled with laughter, imagining the chaotic scene. "Well, I literally was about to die," Rowena chimed in, gingerly touching her swollen lips. "Note to self: always ask about zombie makeup ingredients before French kissing them. Stupid allergies."

"At least your guy didn't ditch you to make out with a sexy vampire," I added, rolling my eyes.

"Yeah." Rowena sighed. "But I don't think I'm getting a second date after the bloating face and blistering lips reaction."

We all burst out laughing, the disappointments of the night fading away. There, in that cozy vinyl booth, something just clicked.

"Thanks to *Legally Blonde*," Hunter declared, fluffing her damp pink jacket. "It led me to you two. Screw those dumb boys and lame parties. This, right here? Infinitely better."

Rowena raised her mug. "Hear, hear! To new friends and crappy exes!"

"And killer costumes!" I added with a grin.

We clinked mugs, dissolving into another fit of laughter. I remember thinking that whatever hardships the future held, I could handle them with these two by my side.

Smiling, I stand up and pick up the graduation photo, tracing our younger, beaming faces. Marveling at how our bond has only improved over the years. Gosh, I wish they could be here now, too, to help me face Tristan.

But, unfortunately, this time I have to do deal with the Prince of Darkness alone. I spend a moment centering myself before heading downstairs, determined to make it through this meal without falling deeper under Tristan Montgomery's thrall.

I take a seat at the head of the table, and my heart sinks as Tristan slides into the chair on my right, shooting me a devilish grin, while Dad takes the spot on my left.

As Mom serves up heaping plates of meatloaf and vegetables, I focus all my energy on not brushing against Tristan's leg under the table. But it's impossible. The electric current that zings through me every time we touch is undeniable.

Tristan finds my eyes, his blue gaze smoldering. I quickly look away, stabbing a carrot with more force than necessary. I feel him watching me, his stare burning into the side of my face.

My phone buzzes on the table, and I glance down to see a new message from the Prince of Darkness. Before I can hide the notification, Tristan's eyes flicker to the contact name on the screen then snap back to me. My cheeks flame, I want to disappear into a hole.

But before I do, I need to at least read what he wrote.

THE PRINCE OF DARKNESS

You look preoccupied tonight, Thompson

Another text arrives on the tail of the first one.

THE PRINCE OF DARKNESS

I hope I'm not the one making you blush

I nearly choke on the carrot, earning a concerned look from Mom. "You okay, sweetie?"

"Fine," I croak, avoiding Tristan's knowing smirk. "Just went down the wrong pipe."

The rest of the meal is an exquisite torture, trying to act normal while Tristan's presence consumes me. By the time we're clearing the dishes, my nerves are frayed to breaking point.

I escape to the living room, hoping a mindless Christmas movie will provide some distraction. But as the family settles in, Tristan claims the spot next to me on the couch, his thigh pressing against mine.

I sit ramrod straight, hardly daring to breathe. The movie plays, but I don't absorb a single scene, too hyperaware of Tristan's proximity. He finds the most creative ways to plague me with stolen touches. First, it's the brush of his hand against my side as he stores his phone in a pocket. Then it's the way his hand "accidentally" grazes mine in the popcorn bowl, lingering just a fraction too long to be unintentional. After that, it's the slow drag of his foot, inching closer to my own until our ankles are entwined. Each contact sends a jolt through my system, and I silently curse him for his subtle mastery of this silent game we're playing.

When the credits roll, I mumble a quick goodnight and flee upstairs, my mind spinning. I claim first use of the shared bathroom and then entrench myself in my room. Not that being here has kept me safe before. Should I lock the door? For whatever reason, I don't.

I pace the floor, waiting, wondering. Will he show up unannounced again? Kiss me? Half an hour ticks by, and there's no sign of Tristan. I change into my PJs and slump onto my bed, oddly disappointed. Maybe it was all just a game to him after all.

I'm staring murder at the ceiling when I hear a soft knock. I freeze, suddenly on high alert. My first instinct is to look at the door, but as a second knock sounds, I can pinpoint the noise coming from behind my head. From the wall I share with Tristan's room. I stare at it, indecision tightening my muscles.

What do I do? Without thinking of the consequences, I knock back, two quick raps. Did I just sign my soul away to the devil with a knock on a wall? I don't know what I expect in response. For my door to burst open and for Tristan to charge inside and ravish me or for nothing at all.

Instead, my phone lights up with an incoming text.

PRINCE CHARMING

Why, Thompson, lying in bed awake at night thinking about me?

16

TRISTAN

I stare up at the ceiling, my phone resting on my chest as I wait for Nina's reply. Each second ticks by agonizingly slowly, stretching into an eternity. I know this is a bad idea, texting her like this.

But she's become a green ocean I'm willing to drown in. It will hurt. I can already feel the air missing from my lungs. I don't care.

I can't help myself. Nina has burrowed her way under my skin and taken up permanent residence in my thoughts. Staying away from her is impossible, even if I wanted to. Which I don't. Not anymore.

My phone buzzes and I jolt upright, snatching it up. I read Nina's text and a surprised laugh bursts out of me.

> DYLAN'S SISTER
>
> Looks like you're the one lying in bed thinking about me, Montgomery

I can practically hear the sassy lilt of her voice.
Another text pings in right after.

DYLAN'S SISTER

> How the hell did you get into my phone and change your contact name to Prince Charming? Are you some kind of secret agent?

I grin, shaking my head while I debate how to respond, fingers hovering over the screen. Do I tell her the truth—that I've been around her long enough to know her passcode to everything is 1389 and changed it while she was in the bathroom? Or spin an elaborate story about being a covert operative?

I opt for somewhere in between, texting back:

TRISTAN

> If I told you, I'd have to kill you. Except I'd hate to deprive the world of your sunny personality and charming insults. Though it seems like you spend an awful lot of time pondering my many titles and thinking about me...

I hit send and flop back on the bed, still grinning. Gosh, I love messing with her.

I stare at the chat on my phone and something feels wrong. Probably because Dylan's name is all over it. I flinch at seeing my betrayal of my best friend spelled in black on white. But I can't think like that at the moment, I need to separate the woman I'm flirting with from the concept of her being Dylan's sister.

I open Nina's contact and debate how to change it. Nina Thompson? Just Nina? Something more flirtatious, even if it's just for me? In the end, I go with Princess of Troubles.

My phone buzzes again the moment I hit save on the new contact name.

PRINCESS OF TROUBLES

> In your dreams, Montgomery

> The only time I waste a single brain cell on you is when my idiot brother forces us together to ruin my Christmas

I chuckle, recalling our earlier encounter in her closet. The cramped space, our bodies brushing against each other as she reached above me... The molten look in her eyes as I touched her.

TRISTAN

> Really?

I text back, emboldened.

TRISTAN

> Because from the way you were looking at me in that closet, Christmas seemed anything but ruined... In fact, you appeared quite... happy with me?

Her reply is scathing.

PRINCESS OF TROUBLES

> Do not flatter yourself, Tristan. You have a pretty face and know how to use it, but that doesn't mean you can do whatever you want

TRISTAN

> I only want to do what you want me to do

> What is that, Princess, because your mouth says one thing but your eyes tell a whole different story

PRINCESS OF TROUBLES

> Why did you stop calling me Gremlin?

The change of subject is so abrupt that I almost fall off the bed. Her text stops me cold.

Seven insignificant words, but they land with the impact of a grenade. As I stare at the text on my phone, my stomach knots tight. It seems like a straightforward question, but coming from Nina, it feels loaded.

Weighted.

I could deflect, brush it off with a joke. Keep things superficial between us. The smart move when she's Dylan's younger sister. But that's not what she's asking. Not what she wants. Nina wants me to be real. She wants me to peel away a layer I'm not sure I'm ready to expose. But admitting why I stopped means acknowledging this growing attraction. This intensity that's pulling me into her orbit like never before. It terrifies me.

Because it's not just physical. I felt it in the closet. Yeah, I had my hands on her flesh, but it didn't even compare to what looking into her eyes did to me. That soul-deep connection. The sense that this woman could wreck me and I'd beg her for more.

My thumbs hover over the keypad, uncertain. I know my next words could change everything. Define a new path.

I could go halfway again. But I don't want halfway.

I want everything.

I want real.

I want her.

With a jolt of adrenaline, I type the truest words I've ever sent.

TRISTAN

> In all these years, I never realized the name was hurtful to you. I thought it was just an inside joke between us. I never wanted to harm you or mock your body. I'm sorry if I did. I'm sorry if it hurt you

My thumb trembles as I hit send, launching my heart into the unknown.

The check marks appear. She's read it.

Then... nothing.

The typing bubble doesn't appear. No incoming text. Just silence as heavy as the words I put out there.

Seconds drag into a minute. Then another. I stare at her name on the screen until it blurs, willing a response to appear.

But there's only the maddening "Read 10.48 p.m." staring back at me.

Doubt creeps in, cold and insidious. Did I misread things? Come on too strong? Is she laughing at my vulnerability right now?

I toss the phone aside and pace the room, hands raking through my hair. I'm unraveling, desperate for a reaction. Any reaction.

But Nina stays silent.

And it's driving me crazy. I can't take this anymore. I need to see her face, gauge if I've royally screwed this up. Texting is torture.

Before I can second guess myself, I'm yanking open my bedroom door, ready to stride down the hall with single-minded purpose.

I don't care if Dylan sees me. Or if this is a mistake. All I care about is getting to Nina.

Demanding answers in person, even if I dread what they might be. Because not knowing is far worse.

I'm risking it all, but she's worth the risk.

I just hope I haven't destroyed us before we've even begun.

17

NINA

I stare at Tristan's message, the words burning into my brain. Putting an ever-increasing pressure in my skull as I re-read his confession for the millionth time.

In all these years, I never realized the name was hurtful to you. I thought it was just an inside joke between us. I never wanted to harm you or mock your body. I'm sorry if I did. I'm sorry if it hurt you

Can I trust him? After all these years of teasing remarks and animosity, could he really never have understood how upsetting it was for me? I chew my bottom lip, composing a million different replies in my head. But none of them feel right. I need to see his face and look into those mesmerizing blue eyes as he tells me how he really feels.

Before I can question the impulse, I leap out of bed and march to my bedroom door, swinging it open. Just as I step into the hall-way, Tristan's door creaks open. And even if I'm standing on solid ground, I feel like a pebble suddenly kicked off a cliff. There he stands, looking unfairly gorgeous with his tousled dark hair and a belligerent look on his face. Something else simmers there too, an intensity that sends chills skittering across my skin and warmth flooding through my veins.

He's wearing only a white T-shirt that stretches over his broad chest and a pair of gray sweatpants that hang scandalously low on his hips. My eyes linger for a second too long before I snap them back up to his face, my skin prickling. I'm suddenly very conscious I got out of my room clad in unicorn-print PJs and no bra. What was I thinking?

"Going somewhere?" Tristan purrs, a smug smile tugging at his mouth as he leans against the doorframe.

Crap, I wanted to confront him about his text. But now that I see him, I panic. Quick, Nina, think! "Um, just heading to the bathroom," I say a little too brightly. Smooth. "What about you?" I ask, trying to act casual.

His eyes rake over me in a slow, assessing manner that makes my toes curl. "Same thing."

We stand there staring at each other in a silent battle of wits. Then Tristan quirks an eyebrow and gestures gallantly with one arm. "Please, ladies first."

I head for the bathroom, hyperaware of him watching my every step. Even when I move past him, I still feel his eyes burning holes into my back.

I duck into the bathroom, berating myself for chickening out. Turning on the faucet, I splash cold water on the heated skin of my face, trying to calm my racing pulse. My mind whirls with indecision. When I come out of here, do I corner him and demand answers about that text? Or make a strategic retreat to my room and avoid... whatever is happening between us? Come on, Nina, put your big-girl pants on and just talk to the guy.

Nodding at my reflection, I take a deep breath and exit the

bathroom. Tristan's still there, lounging against his doorframe like he owns the place, those piercing blue eyes trained on me intently. My determination quivers.

Okay, maybe I'm not quite ready for that talk after all. I offer him a quick, nervous smile and start edging past him toward my bedroom door. I've almost made it when Tristan's hand darts out, his fingers gently encircling my wrist.

"You never responded to my text," he breathes, his thumb lightly caressing my racing pulse point.

I freeze, skin burning at his touch. Slowly, I turn to face him fully, his hand still on my wrist. "I... I don't know what you want me to say, Tristan. I don't understand you anymore."

He frowns slightly. "What do you mean?"

I jerk my hand free, folding my arms across my chest defensively. "I mean, I'm used to you being cruel. To you mocking me. Acting like you hate me. And now..." I pause because the words are too hard to say, they're choking me.

"Nina," he interrupts, voice low and earnest. "I never hated you. And I didn't mean to be cruel, I swear it."

I turn slightly, avoiding his gaze. "You can't honestly tell me calling me Gremlin was cute."

"Why not?" He shrugs one shoulder taking a step closer, making the floorboards creak under his weight. "Gremlins are soft and cuddly and adorable."

"Gremlins are scaly, reptilian little monsters," I scoff, leaning back against the wall, "Not cuddly at all. They've got fangs and claws, pointy ears that stick out, and creepy big red eyes. You can't tell me you thought comparing me to *that* was some sort of compliment."

Moonlight streams through the window, casting shadows that dance on his face, making him even more unbearably handsome.

"I always thought of you like the furry version of a gremlin, the teddy-bear one."

"That's a mogwai, not a gremlin." My voice softens despite my frustration.

"Then I'm sorry my eighties pop culture isn't up to par." He runs a hand through his hair and locks eyes with me. "I never meant to be hurtful and I'm sorry that I was."

The words hit me deep, but I shake my head, unconvinced— unsure I can let myself believe him. "So... what, you're telling me you never even found me annoying? All those years of teasing and taunts were, what, your twisted way of showing affection?"

A rueful smile splits his face. "Oh, I found you plenty annoying. Still do."

My stomach clenches. I knew it. But then his gaze turns serious, almost tender.

"But something's changed, Nina. Something I can't ignore anymore."

"And what's that?" I whisper, scarcely daring to breathe.

He takes another step closer, eyes burning into mine. An electric tension filled with possibility crackles around us. "I think you know."

My mouth goes dry. "No, I don't know. I've no idea what changed."

His eyes search mine as if looking for the answer to an unspoken question. "You dropped your towel in front of me, and I haven't been able to stop thinking about you ever since."

I frown, trying to process his words. "So what, I flash you my butt cheeks and boobs, and you suddenly, what, like me?"

Tristan's gaze drifts down to my chest—and I've never wished more to be one of those people who sleep with their bra on. "Don't sell yourself short, baby. Those are pretty spectacular boobs and butt cheeks."

Heat rushes to my face, a mix of embarrassment and indignation. "Is this just physical attraction for you?"

He takes yet another step closer, his body nearly brushing against mine. "And what is it for you?"

I swallow hard. "I don't know, Tristan. I've spent so many years being hurt by you. I don't know what to make of this new version of you."

His face falls, genuine remorse etched into his features. "I'm so sorry, Nina. I never meant to hurt you. I never hated you."

"But you did hate me," I protest weakly.

"Hate?" He shakes his head. "No. Found you annoying, yes." He reaches out, flicking my nose playfully. "You've been insufferable and maddening... but I never hated you."

"But you always dismissed me like a fly that had better be squashed?"

"Dismissed you? No, baby, never! Do you think I get near hypothermia for just about anyone? Or that anyone else in the world could make me puke my lunch and then go on the Cyclone for another ride?"

"What does that mean?"

"It means you're under my skin, you always have been." His words lodge heavily in my belly. I feel a flutter, like the wings of a trapped bird desperate to escape. "You drove me crazy, Nina. Still do."

I stare into the endless oceans of his eyes and whisper, "So my superpower is to drive you crazy and make you do stupid things?"

Tristan chuckles, the sound creating an air pocket in my belly. "You have no idea."

We stand there, eyes locked. My brain can't cope. When I don't speak, Tristan reaches out for my wrist again, brushing his thumb over my pulse point in that maddening way. "If only you knew all the stupid things I want to do with you."

Suddenly, Dylan's door creaks open, and I clutch my throat. In one swift move, Tristan pulls me into his room, flattening us both against the wall, my back pressed to his chest. He keeps his door almost completely shut with one foot, not daring to push the latch fully in and risk making a sound.

We stand there, rooted to the spot, as Dylan's footsteps echo down the hallway. The heat of Tristan's body seeps into mine, and I'm acutely aware of every point of contact between us. His hand rests on my hip, his fingers grazing the sliver of skin exposed by my riding T-shirt.

As we listen to Dylan enter the bathroom, Tristan's thumb starts to move, tracing small circles at my waist. My knees threaten to buckle, and I pray he can't feel the way my heart is racing. This close, I catch a whiff of his scent—he smells like a promise of dark nights and broken hearts. It's intoxicating, and I have to fight the urge to turn around, bury my face in his neck, and inhale deeply.

An eternity seems to pass before we hear the bathroom door open again and Dylan's footsteps retreating back to his room. The moment his door clicks shut, Tristan moves, releasing me only to trap me more firmly in his room as he closes the door and locks it.

The sound of the lock sliding into place is deafening in the sudden silence. My mouth goes cotton dry as I realize we're now truly alone. No more interruptions, no more excuses.

Tristan turns to face me, his blue eyes darkening as they roam over my face. "Nina," he murmurs, his voice gravelly.

I lick my lips nervously, and his gaze trails the gesture. "Tristan, I..." But words fail me. I don't know what I want to say—or do, or not do.

No, that's a lie. I know exactly what I want to do. And it's him. I've always wanted him, even when I hated him. Especially when I hated him. And now that I *can* have him, I don't know if I should. He's Dylan's best friend, my brother is going to kill me if he finds out. Our dynamic is already messy enough without the need to add sex to the mix. What if Tristan and I end up hating each other even more and really can't stand to share a room anymore afterward?

That would put Dylan in the middle, more than he already is. But it's not like whatever this is will be long term. Tristan is basically saying I'm an itch he needs to scratch. He isn't making any promises for the future. Hasn't even mentioned it. So maybe Dylan won't have to find out. And us having sex will have no consequences.

Maybe the need to scratch this itch is mutual, and then I'll be able to move on and forget him. Give my thirteen-year-old self her revenge fuck and then move on.

No one needs to know. This is just for me. For her.

Feeling bolder than I ever felt standing before Tristan Montgomery, I say, "My brother can never find out."

A smile, sly and knowing, tugs at Tristan's lips. "Find out what, Princess?" His voice is a challenge wrapped in velvet.

Since I don't know how to answer him in words, I simply tug at the hem of my T-shirt and pull it over my head, showing him I'm not wearing a bra underneath.

18

TRISTAN

I watch transfixed as Nina peels off her T-shirt in one smooth motion, revealing her flawless skin and perfect curves, unencumbered by anything underneath. My eyes roam hungrily over her body, drinking in every delicious detail. All the bravado I was feeling just seconds ago is gone. Destroyed by a flick of her fingers. Just when I thought I couldn't possibly be more under her spell, she goes and does something like this, bringing me to my knees.

I'm paralyzed, unable to move, overwhelmed by her breathtaking beauty as we stand there gazing at each other. The room pulses around me. Then slowly, a smirk spreads across her luscious lips. Realization dawns in her emerald eyes—she's finally grasping the unchecked power she holds over me. That teasing little smile is my undoing.

In two quick strides, I close the distance between us. I grab her hips and hoist her up, her legs instinctively wrapping around my waist. I sink down onto the edge of the bed, pulling her into my lap. Her silky hair tumbles over us as I bury my face in her neck, inhaling her sweet, intoxicating scent.

"You're going to be the death of me, you know that?" I murmur against her skin.

"What a way to go, though?" she hums, trailing her fingers through my hair.

I chuckle darkly. "You're enjoying this, aren't you? Torturing me?"

"Mmm, immensely," she whispers, her warm breath tickling my ear. "Consider it payback for teasing me about my ears all these years."

I lean back to look at her, suddenly serious. Being as tender as I can, I pull her hair behind one ear. I watch her struggle not to stop me. Nina keeps her hands on my shoulders, but she can't help the flinch that mars her beautiful face. I hate it. Hate that I'm the one who put it there. Showing just as much reverence, I tuck her silky locks also behind her other ear and then I kiss her there. One ear first, then the other. I trail my tongue over the shell of her right ear, feeling her responding gasp deep in my guts. Then I bite down on her earlobe.

She shivers in my arms, returning the favor as she grazes her teeth over my neck. The move drives me insane. I reach out and gently lift her chin, forcing her to look at me, allowing me to get lost in the green forest of her gaze.

And then, I can't take it any longer. Can't control myself. I claim her mouth as mine. I press my lips to hers, soft but insistent, and I feel her respond with a hunger that matches my own. She tangles her fingers in my hair, pulling me closer as if she could merge our bodies into one. A sweet surrender courses through me as she nibbles on my lower lip, inviting me to deepen the kiss. I take the unspoken invitation, creating a delicious friction that ignites every nerve in my body. The world falls away until there's nothing but Nina—her taste, her touch, her sweet scent.

I should panic at the intensity of it all; instead, I'm smiling into the kiss because Nina Thompson is finally in my arms.

She pulls back slightly, breaking the kiss, studying me for a second as if still puzzled that this is really happening between us.

Nina's eyes dance with marvel. Then her gaze shifts to heated lust. She grabs the hair at my nape, tilting my head slightly backward. "So, tell me, Montgomery, exactly how many nights did you spend lying awake in bed thinking about me?"

She's getting cocky, so I flip us over, pinning her beneath me on the mattress. She lets out a surprised little yelp but is quick in recovering. She flashes me that devilish smirk again and, fisting my T-shirt, she pulls me down to her. I go willingly to my damnation, kissing every inch of her skin I can reach. Her eyes close as I take my time exploring her curves with my mouth, mapping out the contours of her body. I want to memorize every reaction, every sound she makes, every hitch in her breath.

"Tristan."

My name whispered from her lips sends me into a tailspin. I pull back to just look at her. Take in her flushed cheeks, the way her chest rises and falls with quickened breaths, the tendrils of hair that have fallen over her face. The sight is enough to make me feel like I'm the one who's conquered, not the other way around.

Her lashes flutter open as she gazes up at me, her stare slightly glazed over. She's never looked more beautiful—eyes lustful, lips swollen from our kisses, golden hair fanned out across the pillow. I'm completely entranced.

Unable to hold back any longer, I cup her face and claim her mouth again. This time there's no hesitation, no teasing—just pure, electrifying need. I pour everything I feel for her into the kiss, caressing her soft lips, tasting her sweetness. A low moan escapes her throat and I swallow the sound greedily.

My hands skim down her sides, fingertips trailing over her

silky skin as I map every dip and curve of her body. She arches into my touch, skin burning everywhere we connect. I want to unravel her slowly, learn each secret place that makes her gasp and sigh. But I'm too far gone, too consumed by the feel of her semi-naked and wanting beneath me.

The kiss grows hotter and headier with each ragged breath. Her fingers dig into my shoulders, urging me closer. Then they drop lower, relieving me of my pants. We remove the rest of our clothes, never breaking the kiss until I settle once again between her parted thighs.

I stop now, looking at her, asking her permission to unravel us both. She only gives me a small nod before pulling me to her again as if she could no longer breathe without my lips pressed to hers.

We move together, finding a rhythm as natural as our heart-beats, stoking the flames higher.

And then it hits me—this overwhelming flood of emotion I've been trying so hard to deny. It's more than just lust and attraction. More than our maddening chemistry.

Those feelings I've been running from, they're all tangled up in this moment, in her.

She comes undone and I follow her to my downfall in a blast so intense I didn't even know it was physically possible.

Terrified of what this perfect connection means, I break the kiss, burying my face in the crook of her neck as I try to still the turmoil within me, to quell the storm of my emotions. I'm in deep, drowning in her. And for once in my meticulously controlled life, I'm not sure what comes next.

19

NINA

He's sleeping on me. His head resting on my chest, one arm possessively wrapped around my waist, our legs intertwined under the sheets.

The soft rhythm of Tristan's breathing is a soothing backdrop to the chaos of last night's memories. I had sex with Tristan Montgomery and I'm not even sure I can call it just sex. It felt more like a colliding of galaxies, or maybe just the perfect storm of pent-up tension and raw attraction. But definitely not an itch that goes away once you scratch it because now I'm itching all over.

And the way he looked at me last night, the things he said. And the ones he didn't say. There was a moment when I could swear I saw pure, unadulterated terror in his eyes. Is he afraid of me? Of us?

Are we even an us? No idea. I just know that today everything has changed. That my brilliant solution to fuck him out of my system might've backfired spectacularly.

I haven't even moved an inch because I don't want to wake him. Not yet. Not until I've let my eyes feast on him a little longer.

The room is filled with morning light that shimmers on his

dark hair and makes the stubble on his strong jaw almost sparkle silver. The early sunrays dust his angular features with a pearly hue. His lashes, long and enviably dark against his pale skin, flutter in the quiet slumber of dreams.

I lie still underneath him, watching the rise and fall of his chest, tracing his strong back with my gaze, itching for my hands to follow. I sink one hand into the soft hair at the back of his head because I can, because I don't know when I'll have the freedom to do it again.

I close my eyes, relaxing into his embrace, relishing his weight on top of me. I'm about to drift off to sleep again when the quiet is shattered as the door handle jiggles violently, followed by a muffled voice—Dylan's voice—calling out for Tristan.

In a single heartbeat, Tristan's eyes flicker open, his body coiled like a spring. We exchange a look that's electric, alive with the silent communication of two people caught in an act they hadn't planned. That they don't know what it means.

"Wait a sec!" Tristan calls, his voice steady despite the adrenaline that must be racing through him. With a swift motion, he rolls out of bed—the sheets tumbling after him in a knot.

I can't help but let my gaze linger on him for a precious second, taking in the sculpted lines of his back, the athletic grace of his movements. But there's no time to savor the view. He yanks on his discarded gray sweatpants from last night, depriving me of the view of the perfect curve of his ass.

He turns to me, eyes roaming hungrily over my exposed body. Then, with a grin and a tenderness I still can't believe he's capable of, he presses a finger to his lips and pulls the sheets over me, covering me from head to toe.

The world becomes a cocoon of fabric, dim and muffled. He rearranges the sheets around me with meticulous care, ensuring no errant strand of my blonde hair peeks out, no hint of my presence to be revealed to the casual observer.

Under this makeshift veil, I'm acutely aware of him leaning down, his warmth seeping even between this barrier. "Be a good girl and keep quiet," he whispers, a teasing lilt to his voice that sends a contradictory shiver of delight and anxiety through me.

The mattress lifts, and he's gone to let Dylan in, leaving me buried beneath the covers, ears straining to follow his movements across the room.

The hum of the lock disengaging sends a bolt of apprehension through me. I'm a still life under these blankets, barely daring to breathe as Tristan opens the door.

"Hey, man." Dylan's voice carries into the room, casual with an undertone of doubt. "Why did you lock your door? Afraid my sister would try to off you in the middle of the night?"

Tristan's chuckle is nervous, but it passes for genuine. "Yeah, that woman is going to be the death of me." *A good death*, I smirk to myself. A much better one than I would've given him only yesterday. "But no, the door doesn't latch properly; the only way to keep it closed is to lock it."

He's smooth. I'll give him that.

From beneath the safety of my fabric fortress, I listen, picturing Tristan's cool blue gaze meeting Dylan's questioning one without a flicker of hesitation. He's good at this—too good. When Dylan caught us in my room, I couldn't string two coherent sentences together, let alone speak in a normal tone of voice.

Smooth, beautiful liar, I think, an unvoiced snort vibrating against my chest, muffled by the sheets.

"Anyway," Dylan's voice snaps me back to the present, "you down for a run before breakfast? For once, the sun is shining and they've finally plowed the roads."

"Sure," Tristan replies, and I can almost hear the easy shrug in his words. "Just give me a minute to change."

The click of the lock as it slides back in place is swift, my only warning before the sudden dip of the mattress as Tristan's weight shifts toward me. He lifts the covers and dives underneath with me. His hands are on me before I can even gasp—the quilt billowing above our heads—then his lips find mine, warm and pressing, silencing my surprise. The world narrows to the cocoon he's created around us, his breath tickling my ear as he whispers sweet nothings that have the hair on my arms standing up.

"I wish we could just stay like this all day," he murmurs, his voice a low hum vibrating against my skin. "But I have to go freeze my ass off on a morning run."

"Told you my brother was an idiot."

"It doesn't matter, Princess, we'll find another time."

I nod, not trusting my voice, caught in the web of his proximity and the thrill of our secret.

He pulls back, and the bed springs betray his departure. I peek out of the blankets just long enough to watch him strip away the sweatpants to pull on clean underwear from his suitcase. Now I almost cringe remembering it's the same trolley I buried in the snow when he arrived. How many things have changed in just forty-eight hours.

Tristan pulls on socks and running pants next. I watch the muscles of his back ripple as he bends to grab a T-shirt.

Then he stands and peeks at me from over his shoulder, grinning. "Enjoying the show, Thompson?"

"Not one bit, Montgomery. You got it all wrong."

"Oh?"

"You should undress for me, not the other way around."

He's all efficiency as he pulls the T-shirt on, but there's a gleam in his eyes that tells a different story. "But undressing for me is *your* specialty, I wouldn't want to steal your thunder." Tristan's voice is teasing, but I can detect the hint of desire threading through his words.

He comes over and plants a swift kiss on my forehead, his scent exhilarating even before a shower and after a night spent sweating.

"Wait for ten minutes after we're out the door," he instructs, zipping up his jacket. "Then you're clear to make your great escape."

He flicks my nose.

I swat his hand away, feigning annoyance. In response, Tristan grabs my wrists and pins them over my head.

He grins at my gasp, then bends down, his blue eyes locking onto mine. Anticipation coils tight in my belly. And then he kisses me, slow and deliberate, a promise of more kisses to come sealed in the press of his lips. When he finally pulls back, I'm breathing hard, and I'm pretty sure my hair's a wild mess. As he releases my wrists and pulls away, his grin is smug, utterly pleased with himself. I sit up, cheeks burning.

"See you at breakfast," he says with a wink, leaving behind only his scent as he slips out the door.

I bury my face in his pillow and inhale deeply. If this is what selling your soul to the devil feels like, then please sign me up for an eternal sentence in hell.

20

TRISTAN

On the way back from the run, I burst into the kitchen, losing the race to Dylan for who gets back to the house first. Sweat is dripping down my face, and even if I lost, there she is—my prize, Nina. She's sitting at the breakfast table with the rest of the Thompsons. Already breathless from the last sprint, my oxygen intake further deteriorates as our gazes meet across the room. I get lost in those emerald gems that burned with passion last night as I explored every inch of her soft skin. Just hours ago, she was mine, all mine.

Stealing a cookie off her plate, I flash her a teasing grin. Nina narrows her eyes, but her glares have softened. No resentment burns in them now. Only a very different kind of heat and a tender warmth shine through, making my throat tighten.

"Ew, Tristan, you reek!" Nina scrunches up her nose adorably. "Maybe shower first, then cookies?"

"What's wrong, Thompson? Can't handle a little man-musk?" I wink at her before popping the cookie into my mouth.

Nina sniffs again, and I theatrically lift an arm, smelling an armpit. Yeah, I need to shower.

Across the kitchen, I catch Dylan's eye. A silent challenge passes between us. Game on, bro. We both dash for the stairs, jostling each other as we race to the bathroom. I edge him out at the last second, slamming the door in his face with a triumphant whoop.

"Losers wash last!" I call out, already stripping off my sweaty T-shirt.

I step into the shower, and as the warm water cascades over me, I can't stop grinning like an idiot. Nina Thompson, the girl I've loved to torment for years, had her wicked way with me last night and from the looks she was throwing me in the kitchen, she isn't nearly done. And damn, if that doesn't make me feel like the luckiest bastard alive.

As I rinse the last of the shampoo from my hair, I hear the front door open and a high-pitched, excited voice fill the house. I quickly towel off and throw on some clean clothes to go check what the commotion is about. Finally smelling respectable, I re-enter the kitchen, eager to be near Nina again. The delicious aroma of bacon and pancakes wafts in the air, making my stomach rumble. More Thompsons have joined in. Milo, Agatha, Eric, and their two kids.

"Well, don't you clean up nice," Nina teases in a low tone as I slide into the chair beside her. Her hair is pulled back in a messy bun, and for the first time, she doesn't rush to pull it down or hide her ears from me. Looks like at least I kissed some sense into her last night.

"Usually, it's you who steals the show after a shower," I murmur back, low enough for only her to hear. A pretty blush stains her cheeks, and she busies herself with spreading jam on her toast.

"Mornin', family!" Uncle Milo booms, his jolly face split in a wide grin. "Sleep well?"

Nina chokes on her orange juice, and I pat her back gently, trying not to laugh. If only they knew...

"Slept like a rock, Milo," I reply smoothly. *When she finally let me*, I add in my head. "Must be the fresh country air."

Lisa sets a heaping plate of pancakes in front of me, her kind eyes twinkling. "Glad to see you two made peace," she coos, giving Nina a knowing look. "Greg." She turns to her husband. "I think we might have a raccoon in the attic again. I heard a weird thumping all of last night."

My turn to nearly choke on a sip of coffee. Nina's face is beet red now, and she's studiously avoiding my gaze. Did we make too much noise last night? Does her mom suspect something?

Maybe we're being too casual. We went from trying to rip each other's throats off to stolen glances and covert smiles in twenty-four hours. Her family might get suspicious.

I need to dial down the charm—or at least, the visibility of it.

Mr. Thompson, bless him, saves us from further embarrassment by asking, "What's on the agenda for today, gang?" He spears a sausage with his fork.

As the conversation turns to our plans for the day—we're building a giant gingerbread house, it seems—I push my knee against Nina's under the table. She startles slightly but doesn't pull away. Instead, she hooks her ankle around mine, sending a thrill up my spine.

As soon as breakfast is cleared, Agatha's daughter, Zoe, starts bouncing on her toes, her curls flying as she chatters away to Nina about her decorating plans and how to make the gingerbread house more appealing for the competition that will take place after the recital at her school tonight. Agatha brings in the supplies covering the table with house parts, colorful icing tubes, and bowls of candy decorations.

"Tristan! You will help too," Zoe declares, waving me over. "No one can skip."

I grin and press my thigh more firmly into Nina's. She peeks at me from under her lashes, just before she retaliates under the pretense of getting up and doing the dishes. Her chest oh-so-casually brushes against my bicep as she collects the last remaining coffee mugs.

I have to say, I much prefer this foreplay version of our covert war.

All morning, as we work on assembling and decorating the gingerbread walls, the stolen touches continue. Our hands brush against each other more than once, sparks igniting with each touch.

"Hey, Nina," I say casually, picking up a piping bag filled with green icing. "Bet I can design a better side of the house than you."

Her eyes flash with competitive fire. "Oh, you're on, Montgomery," she retorts, snatching up a bag of red icing. "Prepare to be dazzled by my artistic genius."

As we toil on our respective sides, I can't resist teasing her. "Is that supposed to be a wreath?" I ask, pointing to a lopsided green circle. "Looks more like a mutant turtle."

Nina gasps in mock outrage. "Excuse me, Mr. Gingerbread Picasso, but at least my side doesn't resemble a kindergartener's finger painting."

A playful gleam lights up her eyes, and I wait for everyone to be distracted to lean in close, my lips brushing against her ear. "You're good at pretending you still hate me, Thompson," I murmur, my voice low and intimate.

She shivers, closing her eyes briefly. But when she turns to me with a huff, her glare is real. "You're being too obvious," she hisses back, pushing me away.

I straighten up, putting on my best innocent face as I hold my hands up in surrender. "Obviously, I have no idea what you're talking about," I say smoothly. Dylan glances our way, one eyebrow raised, but I flash him a goofy smile that says, "Not to worry," and he quickly turns his attention back to the roof that he is patiently helping Zoe sprinkle with shredded coconut to mimic snow.

Feeling bold, I discreetly pipe Nina's initials into the frosting on my side of the gingerbread house, hiding them among the intricate swirls and patterns. I glance over at her, wondering if she's noticed, but she seems focused on her own work, tongue poking out in concentration. She'd have me fooled if her eyes didn't flick to the exact spot where her initials are, a knowing glint brightening her gaze.

We continue working, exchanging playful jabs and sly glances. At one point, I casually drop my hand under the table and drag a knuckle over her thigh. I let my fingers linger on her, savoring the way she turns rigid in her chair.

Suddenly, I feel mischievous. I reach over to Nina's side of the house, pretending to adjust a candy tree. "Oops," I say, knocking it over with a calculated "accidental" bump. "My bad."

Nina gives me a slight tilt of the head combined with a quizzical raise of one eyebrow, but I can see the amusement on her face.

"Let me help you fix that." I lean in close, under the guise of helping her right the fallen tree. Our faces are inches apart, the heat of her breath mingling with mine. Nina's lips part slightly, and I'm overwhelmed by the urge to kiss her senseless, right here in front of everyone.

But before I can act on that impulse, Zoe's excited voice cuts through the tension. "Look, Mommy!" she exclaims, pointing to an impressive section of the lawn. "Aunt Nina and Uncle Tristan made a candy carousel!"

We spring apart, suddenly reminded of our audience. Our

gazes lock, half-sheepish, half-promising, before turning our attention back to Zoe and the rest of the family.

When we're almost done, I notice a tiny figure nestled in the yard of the gingerbread house, partially hidden behind a gumdrop bush. Upon closer inspection, I realize it's a miniature version of me, complete with dark hair and a smirk. My chest swells with affection. Hiding under the table, pretending I have to recoup something I dropped, I blow Nina a kiss. The way she glowers back at me is adorable.

As we put the finishing touches on the gingerbread house, I bend over, pretending to inspect our handiwork. My lips graze her ear as I whisper, "Come to me later if you want a little more sugar."

Nina's breath catches, and she shudders. She averts her eyes, her grip on a half-empty bag of candies tightening. My pulse races at the thought of stealing more moments alone with her, away from prying eyes.

"Looks like we make a pretty good team," I say, loud enough for the others to hear. "Maybe we should go into the gingerbread house business together."

Nina rolls her eyes, but no real annoyance laces the gesture. "Please, you'd eat all the profits before we even opened our doors."

Dylan is watching us again, so I give her an answer the old me would have given her. "Don't flatter yourself, Thompson, I wasn't asking you."

A shadow of doubt crosses her face before Dylan, from the other side of the table, calls, "Please don't start again."

If only he knew what we're really up to.

The shadows on Nina's face clear and we exchange a look, both of us fighting back laughter. As we gather up the leftover candy and icing, she casually bumps her shoulder into me, sending sparks shooting up my arm. I had this woman naked, panting underneath me only hours ago and now I'm blushing like a schoolboy at a mere brush of her body against me.

"Later," I mouth, holding her gaze.

She nods almost imperceptibly, her eyes shining with a promise of what's coming. I can't wait for the day to end, for the chance to have her all to myself again.

21

NINA

I survey the black dress hanging on my closet door, fingering the zipper running along the length of the back. It's sexier than what I'd normally wear to a fourth-grade recital, with the low-cut neckline and clingy fabric. But it's also perfect for torturing Tristan. And the color is only fitting to seduce a Prince of Darkness.

I shimmy into the dress, the satiny material hugging my curves. After arranging my hair in soft waves and strapping on heels, I appraise my reflection. The tight fit also shows off an eyeful of cleavage, and the stilettos make my legs look a mile long. Tristan will definitely notice. I can hardly wait to see the fire in his eyes turn into an inferno.

Winking at my reflection, I grab my clutch and saunter downstairs, anticipation buzzing through my veins. When I enter the living room, my gaze immediately snags on Tristan.

And the joke's on me because he's devastatingly handsome in a navy cashmere sweater that molds to his muscular chest and dark jeans that emphasize his powerful thighs. His hair is artfully tousled, and his chiseled jaw is freshly shaven.

Our eyes lock and the Earth tilts. Tristan's icy-hot gaze rakes over me, scorching every inch of my skin. The heat in his stare holds a dark promise of all the wicked things he'll do to me later. I nearly combust on the spot.

My bold confidence wavers under the intensity of his focus. How can he always throw me off balance with a single smoldering look?

Tristan's sensual lips curve into a knowing smirk, clearly reading my body's reaction to him. Damn the man and his uncanny ability to turn my insides to jelly.

Steeling my spine, I arch a brow as I brush past him. He subtly steps forward so that my side brushes against his chest and his breath warms the edge of my jaw.

I suppress a shiver, making my way in front of the fireplace where my brother is warming his hands.

Dylan's eyes widen at seeing me so dressed up. "Someone's looking sharp tonight. Do you have a date or something?"

I shrug the compliment off. "Oh, you never know who you might run into in a crowd. There might be hot single dads tonight."

I feel Tristan's gaze drilling between my shoulder blades, but I don't look at him again until Mom arrives, and it's time to go.

As the family walks out, Tristan drops a hand to the small of my back, his fingers searing through the thin fabric of my dress. He leans in, his hot breath fanning my ear as he whispers, "As stunning as you look in that dress, Thompson, I can't wait to get it off you."

I barely contain the whimper that rises in my throat. Trying to play it cool, I toss him a coy smirk over my shoulder. "You mean in your dreams when you lie in bed thinking about me?"

His pupils blow out. "Oh, I don't just think about you in bed, Nina. I think of ways to get you there all day long." The hint of playfulness in his voice doesn't mask the serious undertone of his words. "And tonight, I'll make you dream harder than you've ever dreamt before, sweetheart."

My legs nearly give out. Curse him and his dirty mouth. We pile into the car, all five of us squeezing into the vehicle. Of course, being the smallest, I end up sandwiched between Tristan and Dylan in the backseat.

As if sharing such close quarters isn't torture enough, Tristan takes advantage of the situation. His nimble fingers trail up my leg, slipping beneath the hem of my dress to stroke along my outer thigh. Even over the thick black nylons I'm wearing, the touch is electrifying. Tingles erupt everywhere he touches, my body trembling with need.

I shoot him a warning glare, but he merely grins, his hand inching higher. I almost feel lightheaded, heat pooling low in my belly. Damn him for being able to unravel me so easily.

At Zoe's school, he maneuvers to sit next to me again in the darkened auditorium, but he makes it look like a fortuitous occurrence to the others. And as soon as the lights dim to almost total obscurity, Tristan wastes no opportunity to tease me mercilessly. A brush of his fingers along my collarbone, a hand skimming my waist, his thigh pressing intimately against mine. Each touch is a sweet torment, stoking the flames of this burning attraction for him I can no longer control.

As the final note of the recital fades, I'm a quivering mess. My body wound tighter than a coiled spring. I'm counting down the minutes until we get home, and I'll be able to sneak into Tristan's room. I desperately need him to quench this fire he's ignited within me.

But we can't go home yet. After the performance concludes, everyone gathers in the school gym for a standing buffet and for the award ceremony for the best gingerbread house competition. Zoe wins second place, and I beam with pride.

I'm about to go congratulate her when a familiar voice stops me in my tracks. "Nina Thompson? Is that you?"

I spin around and come face-to-face with Brad, my high school ex-boyfriend. He looks good, I'll admit. His sandy hair is perfectly coiffed, and his light-blue eyes sparkle with warmth.

"Brad! Wow, it's been ages." I plaster on a friendly smile, acutely aware of Tristan's piercing gaze boring into my back.

Brad engulfs me in a hug, his arms lingering a bit too long for my comfort. I subtly try to extricate myself, but he holds on tight. Over his shoulder, I catch Tristan's expression. If looks could kill, my ex would be already playing chess with the Grim Reaper.

The situation is already awkward enough. But Zoe chooses that exact moment to materialize at our side, her face splitting into a delighted grin. She points above our heads, sing-songing, "Ooh, look! Mistletoe! You know what that means, Auntie. You two have to kiss!"

My stomach drops to my toes. Oh, no. No, no, no. This cannot be happening. Not with Tristan watching.

I try to laugh it off, but Brad appears overly enthusiastic to embrace the tradition. He leans in, and I panic. My eyes dart to Tristan, silently pleading for an escape. But he remains stoic, his jaw clenched so hard I fear he might crack a tooth.

I'm trapped. There's no way out of this without causing a scene. Bracing myself, I turn my face at the last second, letting Brad's lips graze the corner of my mouth. It's the barest of pecks, but it still feels like a betrayal.

When I pull back, Tristan is gone. He avoids me for the rest of the night, which drags by in a blur. I go through the motions, congratulating Zoe on her gingerbread house, making small talk with a few of the parents, and catching up with other old friends. But my mind is miles away, fixated on Tristan and the darkness I saw in his eyes.

When it's time to leave, I search for him in the crowd, wanting to clear the air. But he's nowhere to be found. Even on the car ride home, Tristan is conspicuously still. No stolen touches, no covert attempts at flirting.

The silence stretches on, thick and suffocating. I can practically feel the tension radiating off Tristan in waves. He won't even look at me, his gaze resolutely fixed on the road ahead.

I want to scream, to shake him, to tell him he's being ridiculous. That Brad caught me off guard, that I didn't have a choice. But I can't. Not here, not with my family watching.

So, I stew in my own thoughts, trying to imagine how I'd feel if the roles were reversed and he'd had to kiss some random woman under the mistletoe. Yeah, I wouldn't be too peachy either. When we finally pull into the driveway, I'm stretched to my limit.

I bolt from the car, mumbling some excuse about being tired. My parents wish me goodnight, and even Dylan yawns conspicuously. Looks like everyone is tucking in early. Without changing out of my dress, I quickly brush my teeth in the bathroom, eager to stow away in my room. I just crave to be alone for a second, to free my head from the constant need to play a part, before I can go to him and kiss the stupidity out of him.

I pace back and forth for a while before stopping in front of my window. Glittery snowflakes have started to lazily drift down outside. I stare at them floating aimlessly, so lost in thought that I almost miss the soft click of the door opening and closing behind me.

I tense, skull tingling in anticipation. I don't need to turn around to know who it is. His presence is like a physical force, pulling all my strings. Whenever I'm with him, it's as if I've been tossed straight into a hurricane.

I steady myself against the storm and remain facing the window, my senses sharpening as I perceive him advancing on me.

The heat of his body reaches my back before he even speaks. "I thought you might need some help to remove this dress." His tone is clipped, less velvety than usual. He drags my hair to the side, his touch ricocheting through my bones.

I swallow hard, trying to keep my voice steady. "You sound a little testy, Montgomery."

His hands still on my back, near the top of the zipper. "I didn't appreciate you kissing another man." There's a dangerous edge to his words, a possessiveness that both thrills and terrifies me.

I make to turn and face him, but he keeps me facing away, his grip on my shoulders firm. "Tristan, I didn't want to kiss Brad. It was just a stupid tradition. It meant nothing."

He trails his fingers along the upper part of my back left exposed by the dress, the contact feather-light and maddening. "From now on, only I kiss you, only I touch you."

Heat crawls up my nape, small hair stiffening. Does he mean what I think he means? Are we together now? Is this more than just a holiday fling? My mind spins with the possibilities, with the unspoken promises in his words.

But all attempts at reasoning fly out the window the moment he finally pulls down the zipper of my dress, the sound unnaturally loud in the quiet room. The two sides separate with a soft pop, and the fabric pools at my feet, leaving me standing in just my underwear and heels. I feel exposed and vulnerable, but also strangely empowered.

Tristan takes his time, his hands skimming over my skin, his lips trailing along my neck and shoulders. It's both a punishment and a reward, a claiming and a seduction. He's making me pay for that kiss, but also showing me just how much he reveres me. That I belong to him now.

And gosh, I want to belong to him. I want to lose myself in his caresses, in his kisses, in the way he makes me feel. Bold, reckless, beautiful, desired.

By the time we fall into bed, our bodies tangled and desperate, I'm dizzy with need. And as he takes me over the edge again and again, I realize I don't care about labels or definitions. All I care about is this, us, the way we fit together like two missing pieces of a puzzle.

The rest... the rest we can figure out later.

22

TRISTAN

I wake slowly, the morning sun filtering softly through the curtains. Nina is lying next to me, her hair fanned out across the pillow, golden strands catching the light like rays of sunshine. Her face is peaceful, serene, her pink lips slightly parted as she breathes deeply in sleep. As I watch her, that strange tug in my chest tightens again.

"What have you done to me?" I whisper into the morning quiet.

Carefully, I slip out of bed, trying not to disturb her sleep. On the bedside table, I scribble a note on a piece of paper:

I'm up early and went back to my room in case Dylan drags me on one of his ungodly morning runs. Didn't want to wake you. I'll see you at breakfast.

Love,

T

The "love" slips out before I can second guess it. But it feels right. Terrifying, but right. With one last glance at Nina's sleeping form, I drop the note on my pillow and sneak silently out of her room.

Dylan doesn't show up at my door like yesterday. I wait another hour before going down, still making it to breakfast before my sleeping beauty.

In the bright sunshine of the kitchen, I load up my plate with bacon and eggs Lisa just made. Nina walks in, radiant in a green sweater that makes her eyes sparkle. But her gaze hides a certain trepidation as she meets my eyes across the room. I can't blame her —between my Neanderthal act of jealousy last night and the uncharacteristic signature of the note I left, she must be wondering what alien invaded my body.

"Morning," she says cautiously, pouring herself a coffee. Her hair is down, the soft waves that drove me mad last night now thoroughly tousled. I long to wrap it around my fist once again, to expose her throat to me. Do everything we did the past two nights and so much more.

I'm like a man at an oasis in the desert, and Nina is a pool of sweet, fresh water. Only the more I drink, the thirstier I get.

"Sleep well?" I ask, trying to keep my tone light despite the tension buzzing between us.

She blinks rapidly, still looking unsure. Before she can respond, Dylan plops down beside me, oblivious to the charged undercurrents.

"Morning," he says cheerfully. "Leave me some bacon, Eleven, will you?"

With my attention on Nina, I've ended up absent-mindedly hoarding all the bacon. I grab Dylan's plate and transfer half to him.

I sneak another glance at Nina. She's watching me too, with more than just questions in her gaze. That unnamed feeling in my chest expands, warm and bright as the midday sun.

As I eat breakfast, I only half-listen to the conversation flowing around me. My mind still reeling from the moments Nina and I stole upstairs. I'm jolted back to the present when Nina's phone rings loudly, shattering the peaceful atmosphere.

She frowns at the screen before answering. "Hey, Agatha. What's up?" Her eyes widen as she listens, and I lean forward, suddenly alert. "Wait, slow down. They said what?"

Nina's mom shoots her a concerned look, but Nina waves her off, rising from the table to pace the kitchen. "No, no, don't panic. I'm sure we can figure something out."

She ends the call with a heavy sigh, pinching the bridge of her nose. "That was Agatha. Apparently, the delivery service just notified her that Zoe's big Christmas present won't arrive in time. Travel disruptions because of the weather, yadda, yadda... And she's checked every store in town—no one has it in stock."

"Oh, no," her mom says. "Zoe will be so disappointed..."

Nina's already tapping away on her phone. "Hold on, let me see..." She keeps frowning at her screen for a few minutes until her face lights up triumphantly. "Got it! There's a toy store in New Haven that has one left. I can drive over and pick it up."

Lisa scowls at that. "New Haven? Nina, that's an hour away. And it snowed last night—the roads aren't safe."

"I'll be fine, Mom. I've driven in worse."

"I don't like the thought of you going alone."

Dylan clears his throat. "I'd go with you, sis, but I'm supposed to volunteer as Santa at the children's hospital today."

I see my chance and jump in smoothly. "I can take her."

Four pairs of eyes swivel to me in surprise. Dylan looks torn between relief and concern. "You sure, man? I mean, I appreciate the offer, but... you two alone in a car? For hours? Is that really a good idea?"

Nina rolls her eyes. "We're adults, Dylan. We can handle a short road trip without killing each other." She cuts her gaze to me, and for a second, I swear I see a flicker of anticipation. "Right, Montgomery?"

I flash her a grin. "Scout's honor. I'll be on my best behavior."

Dylan still looks skeptical, but he relents with a shrug. "Alright then. Guess that's settled." He points a warning finger at me. "But if there's so much as a scratch on her when you get back…"

If only he knew about all the marks I already left.

"Relax, man," I say, standing and gripping his shoulders from behind. "It's not her you should worry about." I give him a light squeeze. "And I can be the bigger person. Promise." I throw in a little jab so as not to sound too eager.

Nina flashes me a merciless grin. "You mean the bigger jerk?"

"Come on, Nina, play nice," I tease her. "It's for a good cause."

Nina's already grabbing her coat and keys. "Let's get moving. I don't want to risk that toy selling out."

I shove my hands in my pockets, slightly too eager to rile her up. "Then call the store and ask them to put it on hold."

"They're not open yet, genius, but they will be by the time we get there."

At our bickering, Dylan drags a hand over his face. Just as we head out of the kitchen, I hear him mutter, "Let's hope one of them doesn't come back in a body bag."

A silent huff escapes me, amusement mixed with guilt that me *killing* his sister is the last thing he should worry about. Unless too many orgasms are a health concern.

* * *

In the car, the silence stretches between me and Nina as I navigate the snow-dusted roads, the only sound the rhythmic thrum of the engine and the gentle crunch of the tires.

Nina stares out the passenger window, her expression unreadable. I drum my fingers against the steering wheel, searching for the right words to break the ice.

"Listen, about last night..." I begin, risking a glance in her direction. "The whole caveman act. I'm sorry if I made you uncomfortable."

Nina turns to face me, her expression guarded. "What did you mean when you said..." She pauses, worrying her bottom lip. "When you said no one else could kiss me?"

My grip tightens on the wheel. "Just that, Thompson." I keep my gaze fixed on the road ahead, but I can feel the weight of her stare. "I've no idea what this thing between us is, but while it lasts, I want you to be mine and mine only, and to be yours."

In my peripheral vision, I see her jaw drop. Slowly, hesitantly, she reaches out and places her hand over mine. "I feel the same. But what about Dylan?"

I lace my fingers through hers, savoring the warmth of her skin. "When there's something to tell him, we'll tell him." I sense her disappointment at my answer, so I stroke her palm with my thumb. "We don't need to rush anything."

She nods, going back to staring out the window pensively. "Okay. We'll figure it out as we go."

The rest of the drive passes in comfortable silence, our hands remaining intertwined on the armrest.

As we enter New Haven, a newfound sense of freedom washes over me. Here, away from the watchful eyes of her family, I can finally express how I feel about her out in the open.

We collect Zoe's present from the mall, but it's obvious neither of us is in a hurry to get back. Out of the toy store, I pull Nina close, capturing her lips in a searing kiss right there in the middle of the busy shopping center. She melts into me, her arms winding around my neck, and for a moment, the rest of the world falls away.

Hand in hand, we explore the mall, ducking into shops and cafes whenever the mood strikes. We take silly selfies in front of the winter wonderland in the center of the plaza. Nina's laughter rings out like music and does funny things to me.

We stop for lunch at a burger joint. As Nina reads the menu, I marvel at how much I know about her and yet, how little. I know what she's going to order before she tells our server: one cheeseburger with double bacon, a large Diet Coke, and curly fries.

"I'll have a cheeseburger with extra bacon, a large Diet Coke, and fries." She promptly echoes my thoughts.

"Regular or curly?"

"Curly, please."

Nailed it!

I give the server my order, and as he scurries away, Nina's phone chimes with a text. She replies then focuses her attention back on me. She's about to talk when the phone pings again.

Nina lets out a frustrated huff and winces apologetically. "Sorry," she says, rummaging through her shopping bags and taking out Zoe's present. "Agatha needs photographic evidence that we got the right starter chemist set, the one with the pink beakers."

She takes a picture and sends it to her cousin. "Sorry, my family can be intense."

"Your family is perfect," I say, a little too vehemently.

Nina blinks at me.

"I wish I had a family like yours," I explain. "My parents and I don't have the best relationship."

"Why?" Her question is careful.

Our food arrives, allowing me a moment to collect my thoughts before I reply. "I'm not sure they care much for me."

Nina picks up a curly fry and holds it in the air. "I'm sure that's not true. I remember them coming to your graduation, they looked so proud. And your dad gave you the apartment in New York as a graduation present."

"My dad never misses an opportunity to network and my graduation was the perfect opportunity to catch up with his old Duke buddies." I take a sip of Coke. "And as for the apartment, he likes to throw money at his guilt. My mom gets a new car every time he cheats on her. I got a penthouse for my shitty childhood. But it's okay, it was a long time ago."

Nina reaches for my hand across the table, her expression thunderous. "It's not okay." I like that she doesn't give me pity back. Only burning indignation. "Your parents suck, but it's their loss, not yours."

And there it goes again, that overwhelming something expanding in my chest, growing, taking up all the space.

"Then let's not waste time talking about them." I brush the topic aside, not ready to reveal the extent of the trauma my childhood is for me. Years of feeling rejected, unwanted, insignificant.

Over the rest of lunch, we trade stories and barbs with the ease of a long-standing couple, learning more about each other than we have in years. I've known her forever, almost as long as I've known Dylan, but I realize now we've never really talked before. Not like today. I might've learned mundane things about her over the years like her food preferences, but so many parts of her remain a mystery. One I can't wait to uncover.

As the afternoon stretches on, we linger in New Haven under the pretense of last-minute Christmas shopping. But all too soon, the sun begins to dip below the horizon, painting the sky in vivid shades of orange and pink. I glance at my watch and sigh, realizing we can't put off the inevitable any longer. "We should probably head back," I say, the idea of having to restrain myself from touching her whenever I want almost unbearable.

Nina nods, the light in her eyes dimming slightly. "I suppose you're right." She tucks a stray blonde lock behind her ear, and my fingers itch to trace the delicate shell of it—with the tip of my finger, with my mouth, with my teeth.

We walk back to the car in silence, our joined hands swinging between us. The weight of the cloak-and-dagger act that awaits us at home hangs over our heads, but I refuse to let it dim the perfect day we've shared. And the covert flirting is not all bad, there's an added thrill to it.

As we pull out of the parking lot and onto the highway, I reach over and take Nina's hand in mine once more. "Thank you for today," I murmur, rubbing my thumb over her knuckles. "I can't remember the last time I had this much fun."

She beams at me, and even in the fading light, it's brighter than the sun. "Me neither. It was like we were in our own little world."

But with every mile that brings us closer to home, that world begins to shrink. The uninhibited laughter and casual touches that came so naturally in New Haven are replaced by the knowledge that we'll soon have to slip back into our carefully crafted roles.

I clear my throat, trying to shake off the unease that's settled in my gut. "So, what's the plan when we get back?"

Nina sucks her bottom lip between her teeth, a habit I've come to recognize as a sign of nerves. "I guess we just act normal. Like nothing's changed."

The words are a punch to the gut, even though I know she doesn't mean them the way they sound. Because everything has changed, and there's no going back now.

I swallow hard and force a smile. "Right. Normal." I give her hand a reassuring squeeze before reluctantly letting go as we turn onto the familiar street leading to her family's house.

As I put the car in park and kill the engine, I allow myself one last moment of weakness. I lean over and press a soft kiss to Nina's lips, pouring every ounce of longing and affection into the gentle caress. "Until tonight," I whisper against her mouth.

She nods, her eyes shining with a mixture of desire and anticipation. "Until tonight."

And then we're stepping out of the car and back into the real world, the magic of our day in New Haven fading. But as we walk up the path to the front door, our hands brushing with each step, I cling to the promise of what's coming—the stolen moments and secret touches that will sustain me until I can hold her in my arms again. Just a few hours until it gets dark.

23

NINA

A cherished Thompson siblings' tradition on the night before Christmas is for Dylan and me to volunteer to serve hot chocolate at our parish church before the midnight mass. And this year is no different. Well, with the exception that Tristan has joined in.

As we arrive just after ten, the church's stained-glass windows cast a kaleidoscope of colors onto the pristine snow of the courtyard. I inhale deeply, taking in the scent of pine and wood-smoke that fills the crisp winter air.

Inside the church, the warm glow of candlelight greets us, along with familiar faces from neighbors and friends. Mom and Dad stay behind to catch up with their buddies while Dylan, Tristan, and I deviate to the refectory where we'll be working before mass.

The dining hall is aglow with twinkling lights and festive garlands. We take positions behind a long table laden with steaming urns of hot chocolate. The air is thick with the sweet aroma of cocoa butter and the excited chatter of the congregation as they file in from the cold. I scoop the rich, velvety liquid into

Santa-themed paper cups, enjoying the simple act of spreading the holiday cheer.

Next to me, Tristan is doing the same, his dark hair falling over his brow as he bends to pour. As our first customers arrive, I marvel at the easy way he interacts with everyone who approaches. Gone is the aloof, sarcastic man I've known for years. In his place is someone warm and kind, whose laugh lines appear as he smiles.

"Merry Christmas!" Tristan says brightly to an elderly woman bundled up in a puffy red coat. "One hot chocolate coming right up. Would you like marshmallows with that?"

"Oh, yes, please!" she replies, her wrinkled face breaking into a delighted grin. "You're such a dear. Bless you!"

I watch as Tristan carefully drops a generous handful of mini marshmallows into her cup before handing it over. The woman clasps his hand between her own with a grateful pat.

"Thank you, young man. It's so nice to see a new face volunteering. You have such a good heart."

"Oh, it's nothing." Tristan ducks his head, almost bashfully, and busies himself preparing the next cup.

As the old lady toddles off, Tristan glances my way and catches me staring. One dark eyebrow quirks up. "See something you like, Thompson?"

My cheeks heat and I quickly busy myself with the hot chocolate. "Just surprised to see you acting like a decent human being for once, Montgomery," I say more for Dylan's benefit. My brother is distributing chocolates on my other side.

"I'm full of surprises." Tristan's voice is low and teasing, sending little jolts of current through me.

I risk another peek at him from under my lashes. That easy grin is still in place, but his eyes shine with something deeper, something that causes a flutter of excitement to dance under my skin.

As the night progresses, I keep stealing glances at him. I've known Tristan for years, ever since he and Dylan became attached at the hip in college. But I've never seen this kinder, playful version of him. How he connects with every single one of his "customers," from the tiniest toddler to the most loquacious elder, leaves me in awe. I try to puzzle out how he behaved the other years he's been staying with us for the holidays, but I can't seem to remember. In the past, I must've either kept my distance or my judgment must've been clouded by a mist of resentment.

But now that I'm close and definitely not in hate with him anymore, I can take it all in.

His patience never wavers, even as Mrs. Harrington launches into a lengthy tale about her prized petunias. I've always thought of Tristan as aloof, untouchable—the golden boy who could do no wrong in my brother's eyes. But watching him tonight, I realize there's so much more to him than meets the eye. The genuine warmth in his smile, the gentle way he listens to each person's story... it's a side of him I've never witnessed before.

Needing a moment to collect myself, I turn to grab more marshmallows from the bag behind me. Swinging back toward the table, I'm startled to find old Mr. Larson standing right in front of me, his wrinkled face expectant.

"Nina, my girl!" he says, his voice slightly too loud. "Pour me a cup of that delicious chocolate, would you? And don't be stingy with the marshmallows!"

"Of course, Mr. Larson," I reply with a smile, quickly filling his mug. "There you go. Enjoy!"

As I hand it over, my fingers brush his papery skin. Mr. Larson leans in conspiratorially.

"I remember when you and your brother were just little things," he says, eyes twinkling. "Told your parents then that you'd grow up to be a heartbreaker. And look at you now!"

"Oh, I don't know about that..." I deflect, intensely aware of Tristan listening in.

"Don't be modest, girl! Why, if I was sixty years younger..."

From his station, Tristan makes a strangled sound that might be a laugh. I elbow him surreptitiously.

Thankfully, Mr. Larson gets distracted by the pastor and wanders off to find a seat. I let out a breath I didn't realize I was holding. When I glance at Tristan, he's grinning like the Cheshire Cat.

"Not. One. Word," I warn him through clenched teeth.

He mimes zipping his lips, eyes dancing with mirth. I scowl but can't stop the twitching at my mouth. Something about Tristan's playful teasing—so different from our previous scathing retorts—feels almost too intimate. It sparks a little explosion of fireworks in my belly that I'm not ready to examine too closely.

Turning back to my task, I try to ignore the hyperawareness of his solid presence at my side and the phantom tingle of his gaze on my face. And yet, as I sneak him another glance, taking in the firm line of his jaw and the graceful way he moves, I feel that fluttering warmth in my stomach again.

The evening progresses in a whirlwind of laughter and cheers. Despite my best efforts to focus on my task, I find my gaze continually drawn to Tristan. At one point, I'm so distracted admiring the way his broad shoulders fill out his fitted blue sweater that my grip on the cup I'm filling falters and suddenly there's a waterfall of hot chocolate splashing across the floor. In my attempt to avoid the hot spill, I knock over a metal tray that clatters as it hits the linoleum.

"Shoot!" I exclaim, hurrying to set the ladle back into the urn before I make an even bigger mess.

Tristan is on his knees in an instant, grabbing a bunch of paper towels to mop up the puddle.

I get caught up watching him.

"Keep looking." He tilts his head, one eyebrow raised. "And I might start thinking you've spilled on purpose just to see me clean." He flashes me a playful grin as he wipes the linoleum. His words make me realize I'm staring at him sort of adoringly. "If you wanted a show, you could've just asked."

I join him in crouching on the floor, pretending to be focused on sopping up the hot chocolate with a wad of paper towels.

"Oh, so now I can just ask for whatever I want from you, Montgomery?" I counter in a whisper, not wanting my words to carry to where Dylan is working nearby. I aim for a tone of jest, but there's an undercurrent of daring beneath my question.

From his position on the floor, Tristan looks straight at me, his blue eyes gleaming with a mock-serious light. "Yeah, Thompson, you've got me on my knees and begging, in case you haven't noticed."

An overwhelming wave of heat rushes through me at his words, rendering me momentarily speechless. I open my mouth, but no clever retort comes out.

Get it together, Nina! Don't let him fluster you like this. You're giving it up too easily.

But with Tristan looking at me like that, his midnight hair tousled and the magnetic pull of his eyes locked on mine, I'm finding it extremely difficult to think straight...

After the chocolate incident, Tristan goes back to his station and I resume my serving, trying to actually concentrate on what I'm doing instead of ogling him. I succeed, mostly, at least until a tug on my sleeve from behind pulls me from my thoughts. I look down to find a naughty-faced boy, no more than six, peering up at me with mischievous eyes. "Can I have extra marshmallows, please?" he asks, his voice a conspiratorial whisper. The boy has already helped himself to a cup full of them that he's now clutching to his chest.

Before I can respond, Tristan swoops in, scooping the boy up and onto his shoulders in one fluid motion. "Extra marshmallows, you say? I think we need an official marshmallow inspector for that!"

The child's delighted giggles fill the air as Tristan parades him around, making a show of inspecting each cup of chocolate with exaggerated seriousness. My heart swells at the sight. Watching Tristan interact with the boy, so carefree and genuinely happy, I feel something even bigger shift inside me, exposing a truth I've been denying for the last two days.

I'm falling for Tristan Montgomery. *Hard.*

The realization hits me like a freight train, stealing a breath from my lungs. I grip the edge of the table, my knuckles turning white as a wave of panic crashes over me.

I can't fall for Tristan. I can't. Not when I have no idea what his intentions are.

But as Tristan catches my eye over the sea of people, his gaze soft and filled with an emotion I don't dare to try to puzzle, I know it's already too late. I'm already halfway in love with him, and there's no going back.

Now, I can only hope that he feels the same way—and that by falling in bed with him, I haven't just set myself up for the biggest heartbreak of my life. Overwhelmed by these thoughts, I look away.

I fixate on the hot brown liquid before me, steering it as if its ripples could hold answers. The silver ladle clinks against the urn as my mind wanders to the car ride earlier with Tristan. His words replay in my head like a broken record, each phrase more confusing than the last.

That whispered, *"I want you to be mine,"* but that he followed with, *"I don't know what this thing is between us."*

I frown as I dollop a generous serving of hot chocolate, nearly missing the cup. What did he mean by that? It made my heart soar and then plummet as he added, *"When there's something to tell Dylan, we will."*

Does that mean there's nothing to tell now? And what did he mean exactly by *something*? Because apparently, sex isn't something. Did he mean feelings? Are there no feelings on his side as of now?

I grip the ladle tighter, frustration bubbling up inside me. I feel like I'm trying to solve a riddle, but the clues keep contradicting each other.

* * *

The drive home from the church is a blur. My mind keeps replaying Tristan's words from earlier in the car during our day trip. But it's like a Rubik's cube. Each time I think I've figured out a side, a square moves on another and I have to start over.

As I escape to my room, my emotions are a vortex of anticipation and nerves. I pace the floor, my eyes darting to the clock every few minutes. It's past one, and the silence from Tristan's end grows increasingly louder.

I expected him to come to my room at the first opportunity, but as the minutes tick by, my doubts grow. Should I go to his room instead? Are we playing cat and mouse? Is he making me wait on purpose? Is this another one of his games?

Just as I'm about to prowl in the hall, my phone lights up with a message from Tristan.

PRINCE CHARMING

Dylan's keeping me up. I'll come to you as soon as I can. Wait for me

Tension melts from my shoulders, while I shake my head that I still haven't changed Tristan's contact name back to his proper appellative. *Who are you, Tristan? Prince Charming or a Prince of Darkness?*

24

TRISTAN

As we spill into the house after midnight mass, Nina escapes upstairs with a playful wink in my direction. My heart races with anticipation, itching to chase after her and transform those playful smirks into breathless moans.

Just as I'm about to excuse myself to bed, Dylan claps a hand on my shoulder.

"Hey, man, you up for some *Call of Duty*? I'm still wired from all that sugar before mass."

"How many marshmallows did you eat?" I tease playfully while discreetly glancing at my watch. I wince—1.07 a.m. glows back at me accusingly. "Dude, it's late. Maybe we should just hit the sack. Santa won't come if we're still awake."

Dylan snorts and rolls his eyes. "Very funny. C'mon, just one quick game. I promise I'll go easy on you this time."

I hesitate, my gaze darting to the stairs. Nina is waiting for me. But Dylan is my best friend, and blowing him off would only make him suspicious. I sigh in resignation.

"Fine, one mission. But you're going down, Thirty-three." I

whip out my phone and tap out a quick message to Nina asking her to wait for me.

As I hit send, I picture Nina reading it in bed, her blonde hair tumbling over her naked shoulders—she probably isn't waiting for me naked, but that's how I like to picture her. My heart clenches. What I wouldn't give to be up there with her...

"Earth to Tristan! You coming or what?" Dylan calls from the top of the basement stairs, jolting me out of my Nina-induced haze.

"Yeah, yeah, keep your pants on," I mutter, shoving my phone in my pocket and hurrying after him.

As we descend into Dylan's man cave, I vow to thoroughly crush him as fast as humanly possible.

I fidget with the controller as we settle on the sagging couch while the combat scenario loads on the giant-but-ancient flatscreen—too slow for my liking. Dylan throws me a smug grin, and I can't help but smirk back. It's game on.

Soon, gunfire and explosions erupt from the surround sound speakers, rumbling in my chest.

"Watch your six, Eleven!" Dylan whoops as he mows down a line of enemy soldiers in a hail of virtual bullets.

I roll my eyes and hunker down, fingers flying across the buttons. "Please. I've been watching our six all night."

We fall into the familiar rhythm of the game, but my mind keeps wandering to the gorgeous blonde waiting for me upstairs. I can almost feel the silk of her hair, the warmth of her skin...

"Hey..." Dylan says casually, hooking me out of my fantasies—*too casually*. "Have you heard from your parents today?"

The question takes me by surprise, pulling my focus from the gunfight onscreen. I shrug, aiming for nonchalance. "Nah, man. I doubt I'll hear a peep, even tomorrow."

My parents' neglect stings, but I'm used to it by now. No Christmas wishes, no birthday calls, nothing new.

"That's messed up," Dylan mutters, brow furrowed as he takes out a sniper and reveals the real reason why he's asked me down here for this late-night game. To check on me. Make sure I'm okay. "Sorry your folks are such dipshits."

A lump forms in my throat at the fierce loyalty in his voice. Dylan has always been there for me, through thick and thin. Every time my parents canceled a visit to New York last minute, he was ready to take me out and cheer me up. Even when it was the other way around, and I went to California for a planned visit only to find the house empty, he'd fly over at a moment's notice, pretending he'd love nothing more than to fly six hours cross-country for a weekend trip.

During COVID, he stayed in New York—one of the worst places to be on the planet—with me. And I know he did it only not to leave me there alone in our apartment. During the pandemic, Nina went home for long stretches of time, but Dylan never left me. Only Skyping with his parents and sister. If not for me, I'm positive he would've stayed with them. That it was hard for him to be separated from his family at a time when we didn't know if the world was ending. If he'd ever get to see them again.

And when we both got the Coronavirus before the vaccine was out, he barely sneezed, but I was thrashed for two weeks. And Dylan was basically my nurse the entire time.

He's my only emergency contact, for fuck's sake. My ride or die. I go to him for work problems, health problems, women problems...

Well, I'm surely not going to him with women problems now.

The guilt churns in my gut as I think of my clandestine trysts with Nina. I'm the dipshit, sneaking behind my best friend's back.

The guilt gnaws at me as we continue to play. Dylan doesn't deserve to be lied to like this. But I can't stop myself from wanting Nina.

"Shit, watch out!" I yell as a grenade sails toward Dylan's avatar. He curses and dives for cover, the explosion rocking the screen.

"Close one," he huffs, wiping imaginary sweat from his brow.

I force a grin, trying to shake off the heavy thoughts. "Getting slow in your old age, Thirty-three?"

"Old? I'll show you old."

He shoots me a baleful glare and redoubles his efforts, fingers blazing across the controller. I lose myself in the mindless violence, laughing and trash-talking like old times.

But in the back of my mind, Nina beckons, a siren song I can't resist. I need to end this game, fast, before I do something I'll regret. Like confess my sins to Dylan and beg for his forgiveness... or worse, abandon my best friend on Christmas Eve to go have sex with his sister.

Some hero I am.

As the game finally ends—Dylan wins, I was too distracted to play well—we make our way up to the first floor. We reach the landing, and Dylan pauses outside my door, his brow furrowing.

"You sure you're okay, man?" he asks, searching my face. "I know the holidays are tough for you."

My chest tightens. Of course he noticed my mood, even though I tried my best to hide it. I was fine until we served up the chocolates, but going to midnight mass always triggers bitter memories for me. It reminds me of when I was the only kid left at boarding school for the holidays and I was forced to attend alone in that giant, cold church that made me feel like an abandoned orphan in some Dickensian tale. It's a pain that never quite leaves me, even now when I'm surrounded by people who care.

"Yeah, I'm fine," I lie smoothly, pasting on a smile. "Just tired, you know? Nothing a good night's sleep won't fix."

Dylan doesn't look convinced. "You know I'm here if you need to talk. Anytime."

Affection surges through me, warm and steadying. This is why Dylan's my best friend—he sees me, really sees me, in a way no one else does. He knows about my screwed-up childhood, the Christmases spent alone while my parents chased their ambitions. How adrift I feel this time of year.

And yet...

Remorse twists my insides again. Because despite his unwavering loyalty, I'm keeping secrets. Big ones. Like the fact that the second he goes to bed, I plan to sneak down the hall to his sister's room. He's brought me into his home and I'm taking his trust and crushing it under my boots like a ball of snow.

I swallow hard. "I know. And I appreciate it, seriously. But I'm good, man, I promise."

"If you say so." Dylan grasps my upper arm with a firm, reassuring grip. "Get some rest. Tomorrow we'll tackle the Thompson family's legendary Christmas lunch. You know my mom's been prepping for weeks. Remember to wear your stretchy pants."

"Sounds perfect." I force a grin, praying he can't see through it. "Night, Dylan."

"Night." With a final squeeze of my arm, he turns and pads down the hall to his room.

I watch him go, my smile fading. Some best friend I am. If he knew what I was about to do...

Swallowing the bitter taste in my mouth, I slip into my room and shut the door. Only a few minutes now. Then I'll have what I've been craving all evening—Nina, in my arms. No matter how wrong it is.

* * *

Nina

After reading Tristan's message, I flop down on my bed, staring at the ceiling as my mind races with possibilities. The minutes crawl by, each one feeling like an eternity. I try to distract myself with a book, but the words blur together, my thoughts consumed by Tristan and the uncertainty of our future.

As the clock ticks past 1.45, I feel my eyelids growing heavy. I fight against the pull of sleep, determined to wait for Tristan. Exhaustion has almost taken over when the creak of my bedroom door jolts me wide awake, and my heart does a little happy somersault in my chest as Tristan slips inside, his expression a mix of fatigue and relief. "I thought your brother would never stop talking," he exhales, his voice low, threading through the quiet of the room like a secret.

Without another word, he crosses the space between us, each step purposeful, with an intensity that pulls me in with the strength of a black hole—an endless void that will swallow me whole. As Tristan reaches the bed, I sit up, my palms sweating as his eyes lock with mine.

He cups my cheek, his touch sending a shiver down my spine. "Sorry for making you wait."

I lean into the contact, my eyes fluttering closed as I savor the warmth of his skin against mine. "It's okay," I murmur, my voice just above a whisper. "You're here now. What did Dylan want?"

"Oh, nothing, just a game before bed." A shadow crosses his face, telling me he's not being entirely forthcoming. I can't tell if it's hurt, guilt, or something else entirely that I'm witnessing.

"Are you sure?"

"Yeah, it's all good now that I'm with you."

His lips brush mine, soft and reverent. I can tell there's more he isn't sharing with me. But what he can't say in words, he expresses in the way he touches and kisses me.

Tonight, our connection feels different, deeper, transcending the physicality of our previous encounters. There's a deliberate tenderness, a gentle exploration that speaks of more profound emotions stirring beneath the surface.

I melt into the kiss, my fingers threading through his black hair, pulling him closer. As we unite, I'm acutely aware of the shift in our dynamic. The urgency that propelled us before gives way to a more measured, soulful exchange. Tristan's eyes find mine and never leave. In those piercing blue depths, I read an unspoken promise, a vulnerability that we had both shielded from the other.

Each touch, each caress, feels like a discovery, revealing layers of emotion that had been carefully guarded. His hands map the landscape of my body, leaving trails of fire in their wake, and I arch into him, desperate for more.

"Tristan," I sigh, my voice trembling with the weight of my feelings. "What are we doing?"

He stills, his forehead resting against mine as he takes a shuddering breath. "We're falling, Nina," he whispers, his words ghosting across my lips. "Falling into something real, something that scares the hell out of me, but something I can't resist."

Butterflies explode in my stomach at his admission, a mix of joy and trepidation coursing through my veins. "I'm scared too," I confess, my fingers tracing the line of his jaw. "But I want this, Tristan. I want us."

An awed smile spreads across his face, his eyes crinkling at the corners as he leans in to capture my lips once more. "Then let's be scared together," he hums against my mouth. "Because I'm not letting you go, Nina Thompson. Not now, not ever."

As we lose ourselves in each other, wrapped in the promise of a future that's equal parts thrilling and terrifying, I let myself believe Tristan Montgomery, the last person I would've imagined on the planet, might be my Prince Charming after all.

25

TRISTAN

Nina stirs against me, her soft body shifting beneath the sheets. I roll onto my side and prop myself up on one elbow to watch her blink awake, her eyes immediately finding mine. The early morning light streams in through the curtains, casting a warm glow over her peaceful face. A strand of her silky blonde hair falls across her cheek. I reach out and gently pick it up, marveling at how the sunlight turns it to spun gold between my fingers.

Twisting the lock, I admire how it shimmers, capturing the soft radiance of the morning. Then, carefully, I tuck it behind her ear, my fingertips grazing her smooth skin. To my surprise, she doesn't flinch at the gesture. She stares up at me, trusting.

"Merry Christmas," I murmur, my voice still husky with sleep but filled with awe at her beauty in this unguarded moment.

Her lips curve into a slow smile, as gradual and warm as the sunrise itself. It illuminates her entire face. My heart stumbles on itself. I want to wake up to that smile every morning.

"Merry Christmas," she whispers back. "What time is it?"

"Early still. Everyone's asleep." I brush my knuckles down her cheek. "Do you want your present now or later?"

Nina arches an eyebrow. "Is that a dirty innuendo or do you actually have a gift for me?" Her tone is playful, teasing.

I flick the tip of her pert nose. "Get your mind out of the gutter, Thompson. I really have a present for you."

"Wait, what?" Her expression turns serious, and she pushes herself up to a sitting position, wrapping the sheets around her torso. "But I didn't get you anything! I didn't think we were doing gifts. You should've told me."

"Relax, it's not a big deal. Just a silly little thing." I shrug and sit up too, the comforter pooling around my waist. Her gaze drops to my bare chest, greedy as she takes me in. "Although, if you keep looking at me like that, you might give me the impression you'd prefer the dirty innuendo." I punctuate the line by clicking my tongue.

Her responding smirk is vicious as she slowly lowers the sheets covering her chest, revealing an expanse of creamy white skin that makes me feral. "Who's gawking now?" she quips.

I forcefully tear my eyes away from her luscious curves and croak, mouth turning dry, "You want your present or not?"

"Let me see it then." Both our gazes drop to my crotch, and we burst out laughing. Then she ruffles my hair. "The actual gift, I mean. If it's early, we have time before anyone else gets up."

My smile widens. "Wait here. I'll be right back."

I slip out of the warm cocoon of her bed, instantly missing her nearness, and pull up my boxer briefs. I pad quietly down the hall to my room, where I retrieve the small gift-wrapped box from my suitcase. I had it made on a whim yesterday at the mall, not even sure if I'd work up the nerve to give it to her. But in the hazy magic of this Christmas morning, it feels right.

"Here." I climb back into bed and hold out the festively wrapped package to her. "Merry Christmas, Nina."

Her eyes sparkle with curiosity as she takes the gift from my hands. She tears into the wrapping paper with the eagerness of a child.

I watch intently as she lifts the lid of the box, revealing the snow globe nestled inside. Her brow furrows briefly before her expression shifts to one of surprise and wonder. "Is this...?"

"The selfie we took in New Haven yesterday," I confirm, unable to keep the note of pride from my voice. "I had it made into a snow globe. Express service at the mall."

Nina carefully extracts the globe from its packaging, cradling it in her palms. She gives it a gentle shake and watches, mesmerized, as the tiny flakes swirl around our smiling faces. "Tristan, this is... I can't believe you did this. When did you even have the time?"

I grin at her, relishing her reaction. "You, my dear, have the smallest bladder known to humankind. On one of your many visits to the restroom, I seized my chance."

She swats at me playfully, her laughter like the tinkling of bells. "Jerk. But seriously... thank you. I love it." She shakes it again.

Overcome by a swell of emotion, I lean in and capture her lips with mine. The kiss is tender, filled with all the things I'm still too afraid to say out loud. When we part, a glance at the clock tells me it's time to slip away before the rest of the family wakes.

I drop my forehead against hers. "I have to go now."

With great reluctance, I extract myself from her embrace and gather my things. One last lingering look, and I'm out the door, a mix of satisfaction and bittersweet longing simmering within me.

* * *

The morning passes in a festive blur of laughter and cheer as the Thompson household comes alive with the spirit of Christmas. By the time Uncle Milo arrives with his clan, the sun is high in the sky, glinting off the pristine blanket of snow that covers the world outside.

We bundle up in coats and scarves, tumbling out into the frosty air like a pack of overexcited puppies. The snow is a blank canvas, begging to be marked by our presence. In no time at all, a full-fledged snowball fight erupts, filling the crisp air with shouts of mirth and the thud of icy projectiles finding their targets.

I catch Nina's eye across the battlefield, there's a naughty glint in her gaze that untethers me. We engage in our own private skirmish, lobbing packed spheres of snow at each other amidst the chaos. Every hit is a flirtatious tease, every dodge an invitation to give chase. We dance around each other, breathless and giddy, always careful not to draw too much attention from the others.

Later, as the kids set about building a lopsided snowman with their parents, Nina and I fall to the ground to make snow angels side by side. Our gloved fingers brush, a stolen caress hidden by the activity around us. We exchange secretive smiles, cheeks rosy from more than just the cold.

In this moment, surrounded by the people she loves most, I feel a pang of longing, a desire to truly belong. The easy affection the Thompsons share stands in stark contrast to the chilly silences and tense politeness that mark my family gatherings.

When Nina turns her head to look at me, her eyes bright with joy and something deeper, I think that maybe, just maybe, I do belong. That I've finally found my place in the world. Right here, by her side.

But then Dylan decks her with a particularly well-aimed snowball, and I remember there's still a side of this equation I haven't solved. How to tell my best friend I've had sex with his little sister. That I want to keep on doing it, possibly for the rest of my life.

I dodge the thought and attack Dylan from behind. Nina and I double-team him until we all have snow sneaking down our necks and other parts that should stay dry.

By the time we pile back inside, we're trembling, our noses reddened from the cold. But the aroma of roasted turkey and cinnamon wafts through the air, enveloping us in the essence of Christmas and promising a warm reprieve. Peals of laughter echo off the walls as everyone sheds their snowy layers and congregates in the dining room.

Nina's mom emerges from the kitchen, wiping her hands on her festive apron. "Lunch is ready! Sit, sit while the food is hot!"

The table is a sight to behold, laden with dishes that took hours to prepare. Golden turkey, glistening ham, creamy mashed potatoes, vibrant green beans—it's a feast prepared with love. I think of my mother's catered Christmas meals with a twinge of bitterness. Regret for a childhood that was drab and loveless washes over me. Imagine growing up like this, surrounded by warmth and love. Having dinner together every night, then a bedtime story and a kiss before going to sleep.

Nina catches my gaze and frowns at the jagged emotions she must read on my face. She tilts her head as if to ask if I'm okay. I smile and nod because the warmth she's put in my chest has melted all the frost of my upbringing.

We fill our plates and toast to family, love, and the magic of the season. As I savor each mouthful, stories are swapped, memories relived, and gentle teasing flows as freely as the wine. This is what family should be like—effortless, accepting, full of laughter.

After the meal, we migrate to the living room, bellies stretching and hearts content. It's time for presents, and the kids bounce with barely contained excitement. Wrapping paper flies, ribbons tangle, and exclamations of delight fill the air as each gift is unveiled.

In the turmoil, Nina catches my eye, her shoulders relaxed, her expression open. She mouths a silent "thank you," and I know she doesn't mean just the snow globe.

As the last present is opened and the final shred of paper falls to the floor, a sense of peace settles over the room. We sprawl out on the couch or on the rugs, limbs heavy with too much food, as Lisa selects a classic Christmas movie.

The credits begin to roll, but my thoughts are far from the flickering screen. Instead, I study the surrounding faces, committing each smile to memory. This is the family I never had, the love I always yearned for. And at the center of it all is Nina, radiant and perfect, the missing piece I never knew I needed. I thought having Dylan was enough, but as much as I love my best friend, it doesn't compare to what I'm feeling right now.

She must feel my gaze because she turns, her green eyes locking with mine. The possibility of many more happy Christmases together brimming in them.

For so long, the idea of starting a family of my own terrified me. How could I trust in the permanence of love when my own parents never gave me any? But here, at this moment, with Nina by my side, I feel a shift within me. A tiny seed of hope takes root deep in my core, whispering of possibilities I never dared to imagine.

I'm ready to take a leap of faith. To open my heart and let myself fall. Because with Nina, I know I'll always have a soft place to land.

26

NINA

The door slides open with a soft creak, and Tristan slips into my room as silently as a cat. I'm expecting him, but my belly flutters at the sight of him, even as I raise an eyebrow.

"How did you get rid of Dylan so quickly? I thought he'd keep you up all night playing *Halo*."

Tristan grins wickedly. "I played the yawning card."

I furrow my brows questioningly.

"I started yawning—they're contagious and all—until your brother practically begged me to go to bed."

"Devious."

He pulls me close and kisses me, turning me to Jell-O in his arms. When we break apart, his expression turns serious.

"Nina, I don't want to keep sneaking around like this anymore. Dylan is my best friend. We need to tell him about us."

I struggle to control my ragingly blissful emotions so they don't show too much on my face. I strive to maintain a shred of dignity even when my instinct would be to kick my feet under the covers and scream my joy. Tristan wants to talk to Dylan, which means there is *something* to tell.

"Okay. Let's do it tomorrow." Even through the excitement, I feel a stab of anxiety in my gut. "How do you think he'll take it?"

Tristan runs a hand through his dark hair, his brow furrowing. "Honestly? I have no idea. He might be shocked... or he might punch me in the face for messing around with his little sister behind his back."

"Hey, I'm a grown woman! I can mess around with whoever I want." But secretly, I'm worried too. Dylan has always been over-protective of me, especially when it comes to guys. Finding out about me and Tristan... his best friend and the guy I've supposedly hated for years... well, it might just break his brain.

Exhaustion washes over me as I stifle a yawn. The events of the day, combined with the little sleep we crammed in last night, are rapidly catching up with me. "Look, your tactics carried over to me."

Tristan slips out of his clothes and snuggles under the covers with me, pulling my back flush with his chest. "C'mon, let's get some sleep. We'll figure out how to break the news to Dylan in the morning."

We curl up together, Tristan's muscular arms encircling me from behind as we spoon. Cocooned in the warmth of his embrace, the steady rhythm of his heartbeat against my back lulls me to sleep in no time.

* * *

The light feels too bright as I wake the next morning. Did we oversleep? I sit up, dislodging Tristan, and grab my phone. But a quick check of the time tells me the glow is just the snow outside multiplying the sunshine, making it seem like it's later in the day than it actually is. I also remember that it's December 26, which means my parents will leave for church soon, if they haven't already, to help with the post-Christmas cleanup like they do every year. So it will be only Dylan in the house. He might sleep in late. But with him, you never know. He could wake up early just as easily and ask Tristan to join him for a run. Wretched athletic types.

"Come back here," Tristan groans in protest. "I want my pillow back."

"You have to go to your room."

Tristan mutters nonsensical protests, still half asleep.

"Come on, it's the last morning. Then after we tell Dylan, we can stay in bed as much as we want."

The mention of my brother makes him open one lid, his gaze more alert than his sprawled pose would suggest.

I drop a kiss on his temple and slip out of bed and out of my room, heading straight for the bathroom, eager to start the day with a hot shower. Just as I'm about to step inside, a pair of powerful arms wraps around my waist from behind.

"And where do you think you're going?" Tristan's deep, sleep-roughened voice sends heat prickling at the back of my neck.

I lean back against his chest, a playful grin on my face. "I was just about to take a shower. And you should be back in your room."

Tristan pouts against my shoulder. "What if I need a shower, too?"

I stare down the hall. All is quiet. Mom and Dad's door is open, the bed made, meaning they're gone. And Dylan must still be sleeping. It's a risk, I should say no.

"Can I come in?" Tristan grazes his teeth down the curve of my neck and that settles it. I quickly pull him into the bathroom with me and lock the door behind us.

We shed our clothes, leaving a trail of discarded garments on the floor. As we step under the warm spray of water, Tristan pulls me close, his hands roaming over my slick skin. I tilt my head back, letting the jet fall over my face as Tristan's lips find my neck, trailing scorching kisses along my throat.

He lathers shampoo in my hair, the massage of his fingers on my scalp so good it makes me feel like I've been washing my hair wrong my entire life.

Just as things get heated, a loud pounding on the bathroom door startles us both.

"Nina! I need my electric razor!" Dylan's voice, tinged with impatience, echoes through the door.

I groan, reluctantly pulling away from Tristan. "Can't it wait, Dylan? I'm showering!"

"Just open the door and hand me the razor, okay?"

"Can't you wait fifteen minutes?"

"No. You take forever in the shower; I'll use Mom and Dad's bath. Just need my razor."

When I don't respond, he knocks again. "Come on, Nina, open up."

Tristan and I exchange a panicked look. We can't let Dylan find out about us like this! Thinking quickly, I exit the shower and pull the curtain tightly closed, concealing Tristan behind it. I grab a towel, hastily wrapping it around myself before snatching Dylan's razor from the counter.

Mouth parched with worry, I crack open the door, thrusting the razor into Dylan's waiting hand. "Here, take it and go!"

I try to shut the door, but Dylan wedges his foot in the gap, preventing it from closing. "Wait, I need my shaving cream, too."

My stomach drops as Dylan pushes his way into the bathroom, his gaze darting suspiciously toward the shower. Please don't let him notice Tristan, I silently pray.

"Why are you acting so weird? You have someone hidden in the shower?" Dylan asks, frowning.

I force a laugh, trying to sound nonchalant but sounding

deranged. "Of course not! Don't be ridiculous." I follow his gaze to the pulled curtain but can't see anything. Tristan must've flattened himself against the tiles.

Dylan hesitates, his eyes narrowing. After what feels like an eternity, he finally nods. "Fine. I'll just grab my shaving cream and go."

Relief floods through me as Dylan reaches for the cabinet, his back turned to the shower. But before I can let out the breath I've been holding, Dylan's gaze drops to the floor where a pair of unmistakably male boxer briefs are casually tossed on top of my pajamas.

With the reflexes of a jaguar, my brother spins around and yanks the shower curtain open with an angry jerk.

Tristan stands there, completely exposed, his hands barely covering his privates. Dylan's eyes widen in shock, his face quickly contorting with rage.

"What the fuck?" Dylan roars, his voice echoing off the bathroom tiles. He jabs an accusing finger at Tristan. "What the fuck, man?"

Tristan opens his mouth to respond, but no words come out. He looks like a fish on the hook under Dylan's furious glare.

Dylan takes a menacing step toward Tristan, his fists clenched at his sides. Oh, gosh, he's going to kill him! I can't let that happen.

Without thinking, I jump between them, my arms outstretched to keep them apart. "Dylan, stop! This isn't what it looks like!"

"The hell it isn't!" Dylan snarls, struggling to push past me. "You weren't trying out naked yoga in there, were you?"

As I struggle to hold Dylan back, my towel slips from my body, pooling at my feet. Great, now I'm fighting my brother naked. Could this get any more humiliating?

Dylan's eyes flicker down to my exposed body, and he quickly averts his gaze, his anger momentarily replaced by discomfort. "Good grief, Nina, cover yourself!"

He backs out of the bathroom, slamming the door behind him. The sudden silence is deafening, broken only by the sound of my racing heart.

I slowly turn to face Tristan, who's still standing in the shower, shell-shocked. We stare at each other for a long moment, the gravity of the situation sinking in.

Tristan's jaw sets in a hard line that I don't like. We get dressed in tense silence, and then have no choice but to open the bathroom door and face the music.

27

TRISTAN

I step out of the bathroom, anxiety lodged deep in my throat. My heart feels like it's going to beat its way out of my chest as I peek at my best friend. Dylan stands there, leaning against the wall, fists clenched, eyes ablaze with fury.

"What the hell, man?" Dylan growls at me. "What do you think you're doing with my sister?"

Nina jumps between us, jabbing a finger at Dylan's chest. "Back off, Dylan. This is none of your business. Stay out of my life."

"The hell it isn't! He's my best friend and you're my little sister. How long has this been going on behind my back?"

I gape, wanting to speak, but no words come out. I'm petrified at the idea of having pushed away the only person who always showed up for me.

When I don't reply, Nina takes it upon herself. "It's only been a few days, not that it's any of your concern. I'm an adult; I can date whoever I want!"

Dylan scoffs. "Not my best friend, you can't! I absolutely forbid this. It's not happening."

"You can't tell me what to do!" Nina yells, her features contorted in anger. "I'm sorry we didn't tell you right away. But you have no right to butt in."

"I have every right. How did this even happen? You went from hating each other to... to what?" Dylan lets out a frustrated groan, pressing the heels of his palms over his eyes. "I don't even want to know. And it ends now, anyway."

"It's not your call."

"Yes, it's my fucking call, as I seem to be the only person left around with a few brain cells that connect."

"You will not mess with my life."

"Watch me." Dylan makes to side-step her, but Nina blocks him.

"Dylan," Nina continues. "You can't just boss me around. I can handle my own relationships."

"Oh? Ooooooh. So, this is a relationship now?" Dylan's laugh is almost hysterical. He points a finger at me. "He doesn't do relationships."

"You didn't know he was fucking me," Nina snarls, and I cringe inwardly. Wrong approach, Princess. Now Dylan is really going to kill me. But she continues, "So maybe you don't know everything."

"Nina," Dylan threatens. "Get out of my face before I—"

"Before you what?" she shouts, squaring off to him.

"Before I lose my fucking mind. This insanity is over."

"No."

"Yes."

"No."

"Why the hell not? Seriously, what do you think this is gonna do for you? Why him?"

"Because I'm in love with him, alright?"

Silence crashes down like an anvil. We all freeze, staring at each other wide-eyed, chests heaving. Nina claps a hand over her mouth, startled by her own outburst. I gape at her, my mind reeling. She loves me?

Before I can react, pain explodes in my jaw as Dylan's fist collides with my face. I stagger backward, stars bursting behind my eyes as the metallic taste of blood fills my mouth.

The punch rocks me back on my heels, but I don't even try to react. I just steady myself against the wall. I meet Dylan's furious green eyes, so much like Nina's and yet icier than I've ever seen them. When he speaks, his voice is terrifyingly calm.

"Choose. It's me or her. Either way, I want you out of the house in one hour."

An ultimatum. My best friend or the woman who stole my heart, who apparently loves me back. Every muscle in my body tenses, torn between my loyalties and desires. But I know what I must do. Slowly, deliberately, I incline my head to Dylan in a curt nod.

Without another word, I stride into my room, grab my suitcase, and throw clothes haphazardly inside. Nina storms in after me.

"So, you're going to leave, just like that?" she accuses.

I shrug, feigning a nonchalance I don't feel. "This was a mistake."

"You're seriously picking my dickhead brother over me? After everything that happened between us?"

"He's my family," I reply gruffly, continuing to pack.

"And what am I?" Her voice breaks.

I pause, shoulders stiffening. "A mistake. I already told you."

The words taste like acid on my tongue. I hate myself for saying them, for the choked noise she tries to muffle that lances straight through my heart.

I go back to shoving clothes randomly into my trolley, trying to ignore the way my hands are shaking. But Nina doesn't let up.

"Did you mean any of it? The things you said to me the other night, about us?" Her voice cracks on the last word.

I clench my jaw, fingers tightening around a wadded-up T-shirt. I can't bring myself to respond.

"Tristan, please. Talk to me." She takes a tentative step closer. I can feel the warmth radiating off her body and smell the familiar scent of her shampoo that I was massaging into her scalp not ten minutes ago. "We have something special. You can't just pretend it doesn't exist."

Still, I remain silent, roughly zipping up the suitcase.

"I love you," she whispers, so softly I almost miss it.

Three words. Three syllables. They hang in the air, threatening to undo me completely. I squeeze my eyes shut, fighting the sudden sting of tears.

No. I can't let her in again, can't betray Dylan a second time. He's been the one constant in my life, the brother I never had. I already fucked up by falling for his sister. I won't compound that mistake.

Steeling myself, I force out the words that will make her hate me. Make her let go for good.

"Take a hint, Gremlin, will you? This is over."

Nina sucks in a sharp breath like I've punched her in the gut. I'm a monster. She was right about me. What the hell am I doing?

Slowly, I start to turn, an apology on the tip of my tongue. But before I can get the words out, Nina's voice cracks like a whip.

"I can't believe I fell for your act. You never cared about me at all, did you? It was just another of your sick games."

"Nina..." I finally turn and reach for her, but she jerks away.

"Don't touch me! You know, for a minute there, I really thought..." She shakes her head. "Forget it. Just go. I never want to see you again, Tristan," she adds in a deadly whisper. "You're dead to me."

I ache to tell her the truth. That she's the best thing that's ever happened to me. That I'm pretty sure I'm in love with her, too. But I can't. Not if I want to salvage my friendship with Dylan. Already, I know this will be my last Christmas here after the clusterfuck I made. I can't lose him too.

The silence between us stretches for a long, aching moment. In her eyes, I see a storm of hurt and defiance, but beneath it, the unbearable glint of tears.

"I'm sorry." It's all I manage to say. I'm a coward.

"No wonder no one ever fucking loved you," she hisses, hitting where it hurts the most. "You're a bastard, and I hate you!"

Nina storms away, the furious slam of her door following suit. I flinch at the hard bang as if she'd slapped me.

My shoulders sag, a bone-deep weariness seeping into my limbs. I try to pull air into my lungs, but it's like trying to breathe underwater. Loving Nina was never like drowning—losing her is.

Without her, I'm lost. Floundering.

I'm nothing.

What have I done?

* * *

With leaden feet, I trudge down the stairs, each step a struggle. Dylan waits at the bottom, arms crossed, jaw clenched. He doesn't say a word as I approach, just jerks his head toward the front door.

I pause beside him, searching for the right words. "Dylan, I'm sorry. I never meant for this to happen."

His icy gaze bores into mine. "But it did happen. You crossed a line, man. I don't know if I can forgive you for this."

I nod, swallowing hard. "I understand. I'll get out of your hair."

As I reach for the doorknob, Dylan's voice stops me. "Tristan." I glance back and for a moment, I see a flicker of the old Dylan, my best friend. But then he just shakes his head and leaves.

A bitter loneliness clogs my throat. Then I'm out the door, the crisp morning air stinging my eyes. Or maybe those are tears. I hike to the end of the driveway where a car will pick me up.

I've lost everything in the span of an hour. My best friend, my found family, my... whatever Nina and I were.

28

NINA

As I pace back and forth in my childhood bedroom, my breath coming in short gasps, it feels like there's a blade sunk in my chest. Or a thousand tiny shards piercing my heart. The pain that radiates from the wound is overwhelming, it threatens to pull me under and choke me. I can't believe I let this happen. That I let him do this to me.

I hear the crunch of tires on snow and rush to the window, peeking out from behind the floral curtains. A black town car is parked at the edge of the driveway. I watch as Tristan hands his luggage to the driver, pausing before getting in. His deep blue eyes drift up to my window, and I swear they lock with mine even though I'm mostly hidden.

The devastation etched on his handsome face mirrors the anguish threatening to tear me apart from the inside out. For a split second, I'm tempted to throw open the window and call out to him, to beg him not to go. But I can't move, can't breathe. Tristan tears his gaze away and ducks into the backseat. The door slams with an ominous thud.

As the car pulls onto the main road, carrying Tristan back to his life in New York, a strangled sob escapes my throat. I clamp a hand over my mouth, but it's too late. The floodgates have opened and hot tears stream down my cheeks. My knees buckle and I sink to the floor, curling into a ball as unbearable heartbreak consumes me.

How could I be so stupid? So naïve? I swore I'd never let Tristan Montgomery hurt me again, but somehow, he wormed his way under my defenses and into my heart. And now he's gone, leaving me alone to pick up the pieces.

I don't know how long I lie there crying, but when the tears finally subside, a numb emptiness settles over me. Pushing myself up, I wipe my face with the hem of my T-shirt. I have to pull myself together before my parents get back and start asking questions I'm not ready to answer.

But even as I straighten my spine and square my shoulders, I know it won't be that easy. Tristan may be gone, but the memories of our time together will haunt me no matter how far I run. I'm not sure I'll ever be the same again.

* * *

The chiming of cutlery against ceramic is the only sound breaking the tense silence as we sit around the dining room table. Mom's eyes dart between Dylan and me, her brow furrowed with concern. Dad clears his throat awkwardly, searching for something to say.

"So, did Tristan have a work emergency?" he asks, forcing a jovial tone.

Dylan just grunts, piercing his steak with a murderous stab. I keep my gaze fixed on my plate, pushing my food around without really eating.

Mom sets down her fork, her patience wearing thin. "Alright, enough. What is going on with you two?"

"Nothing," Dylan and I mutter in unison, glaring at each other from across the table.

Inside, my emotions churn like a tornado. The pain of Tristan's departure mixes with anger at Dylan's interference. How dare my brother meddle in my life like this? I'm an adult, perfectly capable of making my own decisions, even if they lead to heartbreak.

As lunch drags on, the weight of my shattered heart grows heavier by the minute. I can't take this suffocating atmosphere anymore. And I sure as hell can't be under the same roof as my brother right now.

Abruptly, I push back my chair and stand. "I'm sorry, but I have to go back to New York. *Today*."

Dad's eyebrows shoot up in surprise. "But the holidays aren't over, sweetie. Is everything okay at work?"

I open my mouth to reply, but Dylan cuts me off. "Are you running after him?" he demands, his voice dripping with accusation.

My temper flares, white-hot and explosive. "That's none of your damn business!"

"The hell it isn't!" Dylan shouts back, rising to his feet. "He's my best friend, Nina. You've already potentially ruined our friendship. Haven't you had enough?"

"Oh, that's rich coming from you," I scoff. "You're the one who drove him away with your overprotective big brother crap!"

Our voices rise as we hurl angry words back and forth with a level of vitriol only the people we love the most can bring out in us. Mom and Dad's shocked expressions don't even register as I let loose all the hurt and frustration of the past few hours.

By the time I storm out of the kitchen, my chest heaving and my eyes stinging with more tears, there's no doubt in anyone's mind about why Tristan is gone and why Dylan and I are furious with each other.

As I head for the stairs, Mom's voice drifts after me, admonishing Dylan for his unreasonable behavior. But I barely hear her over the echoes of Tristan's last words ringing in my ears—*Take a hint, Gremlin. This is over.*

I slam my bedroom door shut, the old wood rattling in its frame as I lean back against it, desperately trying to steady myself. The familiar surroundings of my teenage years do little to comfort me as I slide down to the floor, burying my face in my hands.

How did everything go so wrong, so fast? One moment, Tristan and I were massaging shampoo on each other in the shower, about to have sex, and the next, it had all burst up like a soap bubble.

I push myself up from the floor, forcing my limbs to work as I start packing. A sudden knock at the door startles me out of my thoughts. I freeze, my heart jolting in my chest. Could it be Tristan, coming back to talk things out? But no, he's long gone, probably halfway to New York already.

"Nina?" My mother's gentle voice filters through the door. "Can I come in, sweetheart?"

I hesitate, torn between the desire for solitude and the need for comfort. With a heavy sigh, I cross the room and open the door, revealing Mom's concerned face.

"Oh, honey," she murmurs, taking in my tear-stained cheeks and puffy eyes. "Come here."

She pulls me into a tight embrace, and I cling to her like a lifeline as sobs rack my body. For a long moment, we simply stand there, my mother's soothing words washing over me as I let the pain and heartache pour out.

When my tears finally subside, Mom pulls back, brushing a stray lock of hair from my face. "Now," she says, her tone gentle but firm, "tell me everything."

When I'm done telling her about the whirlwind the past few days have been, she pats my leg gently. "I'm sure going to have words with your brother. But if Tristan feels the same way you do, he'll come back to you."

"I don't know, Mom, the things he said to me before he left. I'm not even sure I want him back."

"Oh, huff. Nothing said in the heat of an argument counts." She squeezes my leg. "I'm sure you said mean stuff to him, too."

"No wonder no one ever fucking loved you. You're a bastard, and I hate you!"

The words I spat at him echo in my head, and I feel ashamed that I'd sink that low.

I shake my head. "We were just too mean, Mom."

"Oh, please, if I had to remember all the vicious things your father and I yell at each other in a fight."

I look at her sideways. "But you never fight."

"We argue all the time. And you know my parents didn't want me to marry him at first?"

I frown at her. "Grandma and Grandpa Willis? Why?"

"They thought his job as a plumber wasn't sophisticated enough. Little did they know pipes in houses would keep on breaking while precious jobs like my dad's at the bank could go bust overnight."

I smirk. "Don't tell Dylan," I say, referring to my brother's career as an investment banker.

"Point is, we haven't had it easy from the start," Mom continues.

"But did you ever, even for a tiny second, consider giving up Dad to appease your family?"

My mom sighs—heavily. "Honestly, sweetheart? Yeah. We even broke up at one point." She fumbles with her arms. "Yet our love for each other was undeniable, irresistible, and we found our way back."

I chew on my bottom lip, mulling over her words. They're simple and clichéd, yet they land with the weight of a meteor in the cluttered mess of my thoughts. "Okay, hypothetical scenario," I begin, needing to navigate this conversation like a minefield. "If Tristan and I are meant to be, what am I supposed to do now?"

Mom gives me a sly smile and squeezes my shoulders in a side hug. "Let him stew for a while. If he wants you, it's his turn to fight."

I give my mom a small nod, pretending her words gave me hope even when they haven't. Because it's clear to me there is no if. Tristan has given up on us before we even had a chance. If he even cared at all and it wasn't all just a twisted game to him.

"Are you still going back to New York?" Mom asks.

"Yes, sorry, Mom, I can't be in the same house as Dylan right now. Not if you want both of your children alive."

"Alright," she tuts. "Your brother is as stubborn as a mule, but I'll talk some sense into him. I promise. Now, finish packing. I want you to leave while there's still light outside."

I do as she says, knowing there will be no light for me for a while, only darkness. At least until I have eradicated its prince from my heart.

29

TRISTAN

In my apartment in New York, I stare blankly at the wall, beer bottle dangling from my fingers, surrounded by the detritus of my misery—empty pizza boxes, cans, and takeout containers scattered sloppily across the coffee table. There's a half-eaten slice of pepperoni pizza lying face down on the carpet, a testament to my current state of neglect. The TV is on, the sound muted, flickering images casting shadows over the chaos. But I've lost the remote and have no desire to stand up and search for it.

Three days' worth of stubble itches on my face. I can't remember the last time I showered. But it doesn't matter. Without her, nothing matters.

The familiar jangle of keys in the lock catches my ear. Dylan. He's back home. This should be interesting.

My best friend steps inside. He takes one look at the disaster zone our apartment has become and sighs heavily. Tossing his duffle bag to the floor with a thud, he sags onto the opposite end of the couch, the springs groaning under his weight.

I take a swig of my beer, avoiding his gaze, but I can feel his eyes boring into me, lingering on the purplish bruise marring my jaw—his parting gift from our last encounter. The silence stretches between us, taut and uneasy. Now that I'm sharing the quiet with another person, the car horns and ambulance sirens blaring from the street below seem louder.

"Listen, man." Dylan finally cracks, voice gruff. "I'm sorry I punched you."

I shrug, still fixated on a fascinating blemish on the otherwise pristine white of the wall. "It's not like I didn't deserve it." The words come out more bitter than I intended.

My feelings for Dylan are complicated at the moment. Loyalty and rage, resentment and remorse. The air we share is thick with all the things we left unsaid at his house, regrets piling up on top of the surrounding clutter.

Dylan bounces his knees and clears his throat. "My mom sat me down and gave me a talk…" His voice trails off, leaving the sentence hanging.

Of course she did. Lisa is the one member of the Thompson family I didn't monumentally piss off this Christmas. I don't know, though. If she's talked to Nina, I might be on her shit list, too.

I don't say any of this to my best friend, keeping my thoughts to myself. Forming coherent sentences requires more bandwidth than I have at present. Dylan says nothing further. As if he needed prompting to elaborate. He won't get any from me. I'm in no mood to drag the words out of him, so I just take another pull from my beer and wait, the absence of sound becoming a palpable entity in the room.

Men always complain about women talking too much, but here I am, stuck in an interminable silence with my best friend, and it's pure agony. The clock on the wall ticks loudly, each second stretching longer than the last.

"Are you so upset about me or her?" Dylan asks eventually, his tone cautious, probing.

I don't even have to think about it. "Her," I reply simply.

Nina's face flashes through my mind—sparkling green eyes, golden locks, that infuriatingly sexy smirk. I see all the expressions I've tried to memorize in our short time together, not knowing memories would soon be all I'd have left. The flutter of her eyelashes as she dreams, looking peaceful and unguarded. Her first smile of the day, so full of hope and brightness it could outshine the sun. The melody of her laughter, a sound that could light up the darkest places of my soul. How my name sounded on her lips deep at night when it was only the two of us.

I close my eyes, my chest constricting painfully. The ache of losing her has become my constant companion, like a shadow that grows longer as the sun dips lower on the horizon. Growing and growing until there's nothing left but a pit of pitch blackness.

More memories of us together, laughing, touching, whispering secrets meant only for each other, flood my mind, making it impossible to sit still, but also impossible to move. I can't sleep, I can't think, I'm barely breathing. I'm walking around with a hole in my chest, and every time I think about her, it's as if someone has taken a sledgehammer and battered that hole a little bigger, a little more painful.

A flash of Nina's expression the last time I saw her attacks me next. I see the hurt in her eyes, the way she turned away from me, and it feels like I'm reliving that moment over and over, in a never-ending cycle of pain.

Dylan sighs. We're not used to heart-to-heart talks, but the guy's trying. I'm not. I've lost the ability to try at anything.

I take another long pull of beer, relishing the cool slide down my throat. I should probably move on to something stronger to get through this.

The silence keeps stretching between us, thick and suffocating, filled with all the words we can't seem to say.

Until Dylan speaks again. "Mom said I should be happy my two favorite people in the world love each other, but the thing is..."

"You're not." This time I finish for him, casting a sideways glance his way.

"It's not that," Dylan rushes to clarify, his brow furrowed. "I mean, it's weird as fuck that you two..." He makes a vague, joining gesture with his hands that I assume is meant to represent Nina and me having sex. His face scrunches up, and he looks away, unable to meet my eyes. "That you and my sister did... let's not touch that." He shakes his head. The thought of me railing his little sister apparently too much to bear. And how to blame him? "But since college, I've seen you plow through women like a seasonal latte menu."

I raise an eyebrow at that, momentarily distracted from my misery by his choice of analogy. "Dude, your metaphors are weird."

Dylan sighs heavily, dragging a hand over his face. "I know." He looks at me self-consciously but smiles, an attempt to lighten the mood, however briefly.

I manage a strained smile back, the muscles of my face struggling with a motion that's turned foreign to them. It's a fleeting moment of camaraderie, a reminder of the bond we share, complicated as it may have become.

"Latte menus aside, what I'm trying to say," Dylan continues, "or ask, really—is... what..." He hesitates, grasping for the right words. "What is this thing between you and my sister?"

I turn to face him fully, my expression carefully blank. "Doesn't matter now."

"Why not?" Dylan demands, his eyes searching mine.

I meet his gaze head-on, taking in the concern etched into his features. "Because she told me she's in love with me, and I picked you. Then I proceeded to pummel her heart and say mean stuff I can't take back."

"You can take everything back," Dylan insists, his tone almost pleading. "I'm taking back what I said to you. Why can't you take back what you said to her?"

"Because what I said…" I shake my head, momentarily breathless as the memory of deliberately calling Nina Gremlin, intending to hurt her, slams into me. "I can't take it back. Especially not with your sister. She's spectacular at holding a grudge."

And there it is, laid out bare between us—the magnitude of what I've done, the irreparable damage I've likely caused. The room feels suddenly colder as if the air itself is weighted with my guilt. I lean my head back against the couch, closing my eyes against the onslaught of regret and self-loathing.

How could I have been so stupid? To finally have everything I've ever wanted within reach, only to systematically destroy it with my own two hands?

I don't know how to fix this. I'm not even sure it *can* be fixed. I should've waited. I should've given Dylan enough time to come to terms with what was happening between me and his sister, as he obviously has now. Trust that my best friend would want what was best for me and Nina. But what did I do instead? I cracked a heart I wasn't sure I deserved in the first place. I trampled over the beginning of something beautiful. I left her alone and crying like the merciless bastard I am. She's right. I don't deserve to be loved.

The admission is a bitter pill, one that I can't seem to swallow. It lodges in my throat alongside a million other regrets.

Dylan drags a hand through his hair, his expression a mix of frustration and sympathy. "I'm sorry if I overreacted. It's just… you and her, you've always been so…" He bumps his fists together. I almost laugh. The image of two bighorn sheep bumping heads would be a good way to summarize my relationship with Nina until this Christmas. "And then suddenly I find you naked in the shower. What is she to you, really?"

My chest pulls tight at the question, the answer lodged somewhere deep inside me, desperate to crawl out of my ribcage up my throat and break free. But I shrug instead, projecting a casual indifference I don't feel. "Doesn't matter now, does it? It's too late. You can rest easy, dude. She won't let me touch her with a ten-foot pole after the way I talked to her."

Dylan shakes his head, clearly frustrated with my response. "Come on, man, don't be like that. Please, talk to me."

"What do you want me to say?" I ask, my own frustration bubbling to the surface, a volcanic heat that's been simmering under the cold facade.

Dylan sighs heavily, his next words coming out in a rush as if he's afraid he'll lose the nerve if he doesn't say them now. "I can't believe I'm saying this, but... I want to hear you say that you're fucking madly in love with my sister and that you won't let anyone, not even your stupid best friend, stand in your way."

I gape, stunned into silence, the weight of his words sinking in. And then it hits me, really hits me, what Dylan is saying. What he's offering me. A chance. A blessing. A future.

The beer bottle slips through my fingers, thudding softly against the carpeted floor as I stand abruptly. "I am," I say, my voice cracking with emotion. "I am fucking madly in love with your sister."

Dylan stands too, and we clasp hands, a silent understanding passing between us. "Then go tell her," he says, his expression finally open with no hints of resentment. He pulls our joined fists to his chest, patting my back in a manly hug. Then he sniffs theatrically, wrinkling his nose. "But maybe take a shower first, yeah?"

30

NINA

Cocooned in the supportive love of my roommates, I'm sprawled on our couch in my most worn comfort clothes, clutching a spoonful of Chunky Monkey as Ginnifer Goodwin laments her latest heartbreak on TV—*He's Just Not That Into You* seemed like an appropriate movie to watch for the current situation.

Hunter and Rowena both cut their holidays short to be with me once I told them what had gone down with Tristan. Now Hunter lounges next to me, the carton of ice cream balanced on her lap while Rowena sits cross-legged on the floor, shoveling spoonfuls into her mouth from her own tub of New York Super Fudge Chunk.

"Men are pigs," Hunter declares, waving her spoon for emphasis. "Every last one of them."

"Amen," Rowena mumbles, licking a drop of chocolate ice cream from the corner of her mouth. "I don't know why we even bother."

I sink further into the cushions and glower at the screen. "Because we're idiots. Gluttons for punishment."

My mind flashes back to Tristan's cruel words, the way his eyes had turned as hard as the core of an iceberg while he sneered and called me a mistake. My chest constricts and I cram another spoonful into my mouth, welcoming the brain freeze.

Hunter rubs my shoulder. "Oh, sweetie, I'm so sorry. What Tristan did was unforgivable."

Rowena nods sagely. "He doesn't deserve you, Neens. You're gorgeous, brilliant, and way too good for the likes of him."

I snort humorlessly. "Try telling that to my shattered heart." I gesture at the screen. "This is my future—sad and alone, rehashing my failed romances over pints of ice cream."

"Oh, please," Hunter scoffs. "You'll bounce back in no time. Tristan Montgomery can go to hell and take a hike with all his minions."

Just then, my phone buzzes with an incoming text. I grab it from the coffee table, my brow furrowing as I read the message from Mom.

"What is it?" Rowena asks, tilting her head.

"It's my mom," I drone out. "She says Dylan is headed home and that he shouldn't be standing in my way anymore. Whatever that means."

Hunter's eyes widen. "You don't think…"

"That he's finally butting out of my love life?" I finish bitterly. "Fat chance."

Rowena sets down her spoon. "But maybe she meant that he's accepted that Tristan is into you. That he'll back off and let you two figure things out."

I bark out a harsh laugh. "It doesn't matter. Even if Dylan has gotten over his childish hang-ups, it doesn't change what Tristan did. How he humiliated me and broke my heart." I blink back the sudden sting of tears. "No, it's over. For good."

My roommates exchange a meaningful glance but stay silent. On screen, Drew Barrymore is about to ugly cry at her desk after being duped by yet another serial jerk. I know exactly how she feels. I'm not even sure how I'm going to show up for work on Monday.

I eat more ice cream and sulk.

A while later, right as Jennifer Connelly is about to dump her cheating husband's ass, the doorbell chimes, jolting me from my melancholic stupor. Ah, dinner's here. We ordered three maxi pizzas with every topping to compensate for the Ben & Jerry sugar overload. I heave myself off the couch, expecting to find our usual delivery guy waiting on the doorstep. Instead, I'm greeted by a sight that steals the air from my lungs.

Tristan Montgomery stands before me, looking more disheveled than I've ever seen him. His normally impeccable hair is a tousled mess, his jawline peppered with stubble and a purplish bruise on the left side. But it's his eyes that truly give me pause—bloodshot and rimmed with dark circles. They bore into mine with an intensity that makes my throat dry up.

Shock quickly gives way to anger, and I slam the door in his face without a word. How dare he show up here, after everything he's put me through? The nerve of this man!

The doorbell rings again, followed by a series of sharp knocks. "Nina, please," Tristan calls out, his voice muffled through the wood. "Can we talk?"

"No," I shout back. "Go away."

"I'm not leaving until you hear me out."

I stand rooted on the spot, my hands cold. Behind me, Hunter and Rowena watch the scene unfold with wide eyes, spoons frozen halfway to their mouths.

The pounding continues, growing louder and more insistent. "Nina, I mean it. I'll stay out here all night if I have to."

Just as I'm contemplating how much I'm going to enjoy hearing him grovel for hours—he can be stubborn, but I can be downright unreasonable—a neighbor's voice filters through the wall. "Hey, keep it down out there! Some of us are trying to chill!"

Cursing under my breath, I yank open the door and fix Tristan with my most withering glare. "What do you want?" I hiss, crossing my arms over my chest.

His gaze flicks past me to my roommates, who are now standing at attention in the living room. "Can we talk in private?" he asks, the question quiet but urgent.

I scoff, tossing my hair over my shoulder. "Anything you have to say to me, you can say in front of them."

Tristan's jaw clenches as he takes in Hunter and Rowena's hostile expressions. For a moment, I think he might turn tail and run. But then his shoulders square, and he meets my gaze head-on, determination etched into every line of his handsome face.

"Fine, I can deal with an angry woman or three." He steps forward into the apartment.

My entire body tightens as he brushes past me, his familiar scent enveloping me like a cloud. I close the door behind him with a shaky hand, steeling myself for whatever bombshell he's about to drop. No matter what he says, I'll just have to fend off his pathetic excuses and stay strong.

"I'm sorry I left," Tristan starts, his voice raw with emotion in a way that makes my task of resisting him at all costs already a thousand times more difficult.

But I gather my resolve, determined not to let him off the hook so easily. "Why? Why wait until now to tell me?"

And then it hits me. My mom's text. Dylan coming home. The timing of Tristan's sudden appearance. I narrow my eyes at him accusingly. "Oh, because my idiot brother has given you permission, so now what? You want to toy with me some more?"

Tristan's face contorts in frustration. He rakes a hand through his disheveled hair, making it stand on end. "I never wanted to toy with you, Nina!" he shouts, exasperated. "I'm here because I'm stupidly, madly in love with you!"

The words hang in the air between us, so tangible I could almost reach out and grab them. My heart sputters to a stop, then kicks into overdrive. I'm vaguely aware of Hunter letting out a startled gasp behind me, but I can't tear my eyes away from Tristan's face.

He loves me. Tristan Montgomery, the man I've been fighting my feelings for since I was thirteen, just admitted he's in love with me.

I want to believe him. Gosh, I want to throw myself into his arms and never let go. But the cynical part of me, the part that's been hurt too many times by him before, holds me back.

"Until Dylan changes his mind again and tells you otherwise," I retort, my voice trembling slightly.

Tristan takes a step forward, closing part of the distance between us—at least the physical one. His hand twitches at his side as if he was aching to reach out and touch me. "Leave Dylan out of this," he says firmly. "I'm talking about us now."

I let out a disbelieving scoff. "Hard to leave my brother out when you picked him over me." The unspoken question burns in my throat. Why? Why did he choose Dylan? Why wasn't I enough?

But I don't dare voice them aloud. I'm terrified of the answers he might give. That his bond with Dylan will always come first, and I'll forever be on the outside looking in.

Tristan's piercing blue eyes drill into me, seeming to see straight through my defenses. To understand what I'm not asking, but need to hear all the same. He draws in a shaking breath. "Dylan is my family," he begins, voice even more rugged.

"Yes, you said." Bitterness laces my reply as I hug myself tightly.

But Tristan presses on, laying his soul bare before me. "No, you don't understand. I'd never had a family before I met him. I told you that my relationship with my parents is shaky, but I never told you that I practically felt like an orphan growing up. I was a boisterous child. My father was never home. My mother didn't care to deal with me or my shenanigans."

He looks away, jaw clenching. "I was raised by nannies first, then shipped off to boarding school when I was seven, left there for countless holidays when my parents didn't bother to pick me up. There are more Christmases that I spent alone than ones I spent with them." He loudly gasps for air before continuing. "The reason I came to your house for Christmas this year is not that my flight was canceled, it's that they told me not to bother to go home because they wouldn't be there. In a fucking text. My mom couldn't even be bothered to give me a call to say they were ditching me yet again."

My heart clenches painfully in my chest. I had no idea... All those times Dylan brought him home for long weekends or Thanksgiving, I never understood. I could've never imagined this. Even when he said his parents didn't love him, I hadn't imagined it was this bad.

Tristan meets my gaze again, eyes glistening. "No one has ever wanted me or made me feel like I had a home until I met your brother. We've lived together since freshman year, and that's when I stopped feeling so fucking alone."

His voice breaks and he swallows hard. "Dylan's always been there for me, you know? He never left me. If my parents bailed on me, he was always there to pick up the pieces. He has never let me spend a holiday alone, even knowing he'd face your wrath for bringing me home."

Tears prick at the corners of my eyes. All the resentment I harbored... if only I had known the truth.

"He's been my father, my mother, and my brother since I've met him," Tristan finishes hoarsely.

A strangled sob echoes from behind me. Startled, I spin around to find Hunter standing there, openly bawling.

"I'm sorry," she hiccups, wiping at her tears. "That is just so moving."

Rowena sidles up to her, giving me an apologetic smile as she takes Hunter's arm. "Excuse us, we're going to leave you alone for the rest of your conversation. Please, carry on."

They disappear down the hall, Hunter's sniffles fading. And then it's just me and Tristan, the air heavy with everything that's been revealed.

As I hold his gaze, time slows, pulling us into a bubble. I'm the first to pierce the silence. "I had no idea," I whisper. "About any of it." I'm struggling because what he just said explains why he acted like he did, but also makes things worse in a way.

I brace myself for what I have to pry out of him. "Okay, you love Dylan, but if he's your family, where does that leave me?" I ask, my lungs not fully expanding. "Are you always going to pick him over me?"

Tristan takes another step forward, his expression earnest. "Just try to understand me. He's the only person who's been there for me and I lied to him, went behind his back, betrayed him."

Anger flares inside me. "Is loving me a betrayal?"

He clenches and unclenches his fists at his sides. "The betrayal was not telling him. Not being honest with the one person who's always been loyal to me. So, I panicked, and I left when he asked. I was mean to you. I made you hate me." The memory of him calling me a gremlin stings like a fresh slap. I swallow my tears back. "But it was a mistake," he adds softly.

"You said I was the mistake." My voice cracks, the words barely escaping my constricted throat.

Tristan's reaction shocks me. He brings the heel of his hand to his temple and legit starts to cry. Tristan Montgomery, the most unshakable person I know, is crying. In my living room.

"I'm sorry," he says, his voice coarse like sandpaper grating straight against my heart. "I don't know how to show up for people. I'm a mess and that's why your brother didn't want me to date you, and I only proved him right."

He backs away. "I understand if you want nothing to do with me. If you can't love me. I'm sorry."

As he turns to leave, I'm seized by panic. I can't watch him walk away again. "Tristan," I call out.

He pauses, glancing back at me with so much vulnerability in his eyes that it takes my breath away. I go to him, cupping his face in my hands. His stubble prickles my palms, longer than I've ever seen it on his usually impeccable face.

I search the piercing blue of his irises, seeing all the rejection, the insecurity, and the heartbreak written in them. And suddenly, I know exactly what I need to do.

31

TRISTAN

I turn to go, my heart shattering into a million pieces. The weight of her disappointment, of the pain I caused, it all comes crashing down on me in this moment. I can't take it anymore.

My vision blurs through my tears. I'm crying like a fucking baby. But I won't let her see me this broken.

I stumble toward the door, my feet dragging. Each step takes me further away from her, from the only woman I've ever truly loved. But she doesn't want me. Not anymore. And I must respect her choice.

Coming here was a mistake. To think she could ever forgive me for the things I've done. The lies I've told. The hearts I've broken, including my own. I was a fool for believing we could make this work, that our love was strong enough to overcome the hurt and betrayal—it was all just a beautiful, terrible fantasy. One I have to let go of.

I reach for the doorknob, my hand shaking uncontrollably. This is it. The end of the line for us. I have to walk away now before I completely fall apart. Before she sees the cracks in my facade, the brokenness inside.

I hesitate, fighting the urge to look back at her one last time. To memorize every line and plane of her face, every golden strand of hair. But I know if I do, I'll never be able to pull out. I'm about to open the door, ready to leave my heart behind, shattered on her doorstep, when Nina's voice stops me. "Tristan." My name on her lips, uttered like a plea and a prayer, stops me in my tracks, hand outstretched.

Slowly, I turn back to face her. She walks toward me, eyes shimmering with some undefinable emotion that punches me hard in the sternum. When she reaches me, she lifts her hand and cups my cheek. Her touch is soft but sure.

We stand there for a long moment, gazing at each other in loaded silence. I search her expressive eyes, trying to decipher what she's thinking. What this means.

Finally, she speaks, her voice barely above a whisper. "I don't know what kind of fucked up family you had growing up or why they didn't love you like you deserve."

The scars of old wounds throb dully at her words. But she continues, her tone fierce now.

"Because you're worthy of being loved, Tristan." Her thumb grazes over the stubble shadowing my jaw, leaving tingles in its wake. "And when people love you, they don't just leave at the first bump in the road or after a fight."

Hope flares in my chest, dangerous and bright. I study her face intently, hardly daring to believe what I'm hearing. "What are you saying, Nina?" My voice comes out rough, laced with a vulnerability I rarely show.

Her lips quirk into the hint of a smile. "I'm saying that you made me fall in love with you, dumbass." Her words almost knock me off my feet. I blink rapidly, stunned. "And that's not just going to go away because you behaved like a jerk. And yes, we will fight."

"We will?" I ask faintly, struggling to process this sudden shift.

Moments ago, I was drowning in despair, convinced I'd lost her for good. Now she's telling me she loves me? That there will be fights?

"Yes, we will. And we'll get petty, and frustrating, and unbearable at times." Amusement dances in her emerald eyes. "I'll give you the silent treatment for days just for not putting laundry in the hamper."

A surprised laugh escapes me. Her words paint a picture of a shared life, a future, and warmth spreads through my chest at the thought, chasing away the despair.

I let myself smile tentatively. "I'm afraid the opposite will be true. You're way messier than I am." She's a hurricane of chaos everywhere but at work.

"But we don't leave," she says firmly, still caressing my cheek. "When you love someone, you don't leave." Her gaze bores into mine, seeking assurance. "Promise me now that you won't leave again."

Emotion clogs my throat. I grasp her hand and pull her into a fierce embrace, burying my face in her blonde waves. Her scent envelops me, soothing and arousing at once. "I promise," I rasp.

Drawing back slightly, I cup her cheeks, thumbs stroking her soft skin. "Do you promise the same?" I hardly recognize my voice, tremulous and unsure.

She meets my eyes steadily. "Yes, Tristan. I promise the same." She smiles now. "You and me? We're endgame."

Relief crashes over me, followed by a swell of love and longing so intense it consumes me whole. I crush my mouth to hers, pouring everything I feel into the kiss. Nina responds with matching fervor, her lips parting under mine.

As I rediscover the feel of her mouth, I feel like I've finally come home. Here, with her in my arms, the universe clicks into place. The jagged pieces of my heart start to mend.

Her mouth crashes into mine again and again, each touch

repairing the voids and cracks her absence had left in me. Nina's fingers tangle in my hair as I pull her body flush against me, desperate to eliminate any remaining space between us. The kiss deepens, igniting a fire within me that spreads unchecked through my veins. I pour every ounce of longing and desire I've felt these past few days into this kiss, savoring the softness of her lips and the intoxicating taste of her.

My hands roam her curves, relishing the way they fit perfectly in my grasp. Nina lets out a soft moan against my mouth and it's nearly my undoing. I grip her hips, thumbs brushing the exposed sliver of skin where her sweater rides up. She arches into my touch, our bodies melding together as if we were made for each other.

I trail kisses along her jawline and down the column of her neck, drunk on the scent of her—sugar and something uniquely Nina. She tilts her head back, hands fisting in my shirt. I nip at her collarbone and she gasps. That sound shoots straight to my core. I need to hear it again. And again.

My fingers find the hem of her sweater and start inching it upward, revealing more of her smooth skin that I ache to map with my hands and mouth. Nina's fingers are just as eager, hastily working the buttons of my shirt. We're seconds away from ripping each other's clothes off right here in her living room when the doorbell rings.

I open the door since I'm the closest one. A pizza delivery guy with three larges in his hands waits on the other side, I hand him a hundred-dollar bill and tell him to keep the change.

I drop the pizzas on Nina's counter and I'm about to kiss her again when she blocks me.

"Wait." Nina pulls back slightly. "My roommates. They're right in the other room."

I groan, resting my forehead against hers as I close my eyes and fight to keep under check the beast within me that wants to come out and devour her. Nina's right. As much as I want to lay her down on the couch and worship every inch of her gorgeous body, we can't. Not here.

"We could go back to my place..." I suggest halfheartedly, already knowing the answer.

Nina raises an eyebrow. "With Dylan there? I know he's okay with us dating now, but I don't think he's quite at the 'my best friend banging my little sister in the next room' level of chill yet."

I chuckle. She has a point. "You're right."

"He needs to move out of your place."

"Agreed. But that's a future solution. I need a now solution."

She worries her lower lip in that adorable way of hers. "I don't know." Her eyes stray down the hall leading to her bedroom. "The walls in this house are super thin..."

I move closer, whispering softly against the curve of her ear. "Then I'll have to gag you. Because there's no way in hell I'm waiting another minute to make love to you."

Her eyes sparkle at my words. In one smooth motion, I scoop Nina up into my arms. She lets out a surprised gasp, legs automatically wrapping around my waist. Nina shivers against my chest and captures my mouth in a searing kiss. Grinning, I carry her to the bedroom, kicking the door shut behind us.

We collapse onto her bed in a heap of laughter. But as I stare down at her, my smile fades, replaced by a tidal wave of emotion.

"I love you." I tenderly brush a golden strand from her face.

She traces the contours of my face with her fingertips. "I love you too."

When I still don't move, she arches into me. "Tristan, please."

I kiss her again, slow and deep, savoring each precious second. Each untold promise I can read in her eyes. It's a kiss that tastes of a future together. Of shared moments, big and small. The beginning of a life together made of cold winter days passed snuggling by the fire. Of hurried breakfasts before work where a goodbye kiss is savored more than coffee. And of endless nights spent in each other's arms after a long day apart. I can see us brushing our teeth side by side in the bathroom, fighting for supremacy over the sink. And picture countless weekend mornings, where the only plan is to have no plans at all.

A lifetime of love and laughter, of happiness. Where we show up for each other. Every day.

EPILOGUE
NINA

Six months later

I toss my toiletries unceremoniously into a cardboard box, glancing over at Rowena hunched miserably over the toilet. The pungent smell of vomit mingles with the floral scent of air freshener.

I open the window to let in a bit of fresh air and turn to Hunter, who's helping us pack. "Are you sure you'll be fine living with my gross brother?" I ask her.

She frowns, her dark brows knitting together as she keeps folding towels perched on the bathtub. "What's gross about him?"

"He's a man," I state matter-of-factly.

Hunter snorts. "You're moving in with an equally gross man and you don't seem too chafed."

A sly grin spreads across my face. "No, but contrary to you, I'll be getting a lot of sex out of the new arrangement."

Hunter's cheeks flush scarlet, and she quickly looks away, busying herself with refolding the same towel. That's an interesting reaction, I wonder where her mind just went.

Shaking her head, Hunter changes the subject. "Anyway, you should worry about Pukerella over there who's agreed to marry a perfect stranger and move in with him."

Rowena wipes her mouth on the back of her hand, her face pale and glistening with sweat. Looking up, she pushes a strand of chestnut hair from her forehead with a slight tremor.

"I lost my job, I'm pregnant with my douchebag ex's baby, and I can't make rent anymore. I don't have a choice," she says wearily. "But it's strictly a business arrangement with this guy. Nothing more."

I exchange a worried glance with Hunter. Marrying a total stranger, even if it's just on paper, seems like an enormously bad idea. Especially while pregnant and vulnerable.

"Are you sure about this, Winnie?" I ask gently. "What if he turns out to be a creep? Or worse?"

Rowena shrugs and leans back over the toilet bowl as another wave of nausea hits. Her voice is muffled as she replies, "He comes... highly recommended. It'll be fine."

I'm not convinced, but arguing with her now while she's puking her guts out seems pointless. I just hope this marriage of convenience doesn't turn into a nightmare for my friend. She's been through enough already. But the least I could do is let her know she has a choice if she wants a different road.

I crouch down on the cold tile floor beside Rowena, gently massaging her lower back as she hugs the toilet bowl. "Hey, if you want to blow off this whole fake marriage thing, just say the word. Hunter and I are here for you, no matter what."

Rowena lifts her head, grimacing, her glasses slightly askew. "Thanks, Neens. I appreciate you guys being here for me." She takes a shaky breath. "I don't know what I'd do without—" Her words are cut off by another violent heave. She accidentally knocks over the towel rack that goes down with a crash.

I straighten it and keep rubbing her back, exchanging a concerned look with Hunter over Rowena's head. Just then, Tristan and Dylan burst into the bathroom, their faces etched with worry.

"Everything okay in here?" Dylan asks, his brow furrowed.

Rowena waves them off. "Just morning sickness, give a puking lady her privacy, please?"

I stand up, shooing everyone away.

Hunter grabs one of the boxes scattered on the floor. Dylan offers to take it from her. In response, she drops it, sending a flurry of packing peanuts scattering across the tiles. Her face turns beet red as she scrambles to clean up the mess, pointedly avoiding Dylan's gaze. I narrow my eyes, a sneaking suspicion forming in my mind. Could Hunter have a crush on my brother?

Before I can elaborate, Tristan is at my side, his strong arm wrapping around my waist and pulling me close as we exit the bathroom. The heat of his body seeps through my thin T-shirt, and I can't help but melt into his embrace. Our eyes meet, and he smirks, flicking my nose. "In a little while it could be you puking your guts out with a mini-me inside you."

"Yeah, right," I scoff. "After seeing what pregnancy does to a woman, I've bought a jumbo pack of condoms."

At the mention of condoms, Dylan clears his throat awkwardly. I catch him averting his eyes, still not quite comfortable seeing his best friend and little sister all over each other.

Hunter crashes out of the bathroom next, colliding with Dylan and turning even more beetroot red. Something is definitely going on there.

But to spare her the awkwardness, I disentangle myself from Tristan and clap my hands. "Okay, I think we could all use a break."

We spread in the living room, Tristan's arm slipping easily over my shoulders as Hunter bustles around the kitchen, setting the kettle on the stove. Rowena joins us minutes later, sagging on the floor and still looking ashen.

As the kettle whistles, Hunter emerges from the kitchen carrying two steaming mugs. "Ginger tea for Winnie," she says gently, handing my pale-faced friend a cup. "Should help with the nausea."

"Thanks," Rowena murmurs, mustering a weak smile. She cradles the mug in her hands but doesn't drink, probably wanting to be sure she can handle the liquids without prompting more nausea.

I help Hunt carry the rest of the mugs—regular tea for us. And we all settle once again.

"So," Tristan says, his blue eyes sparkling as he looks at me. "Who's most excited about the new roommate situation?" He grins like a fool.

I elbow him playfully. "You're such a dork."

Dylan gives a small cough. "It'll be nice to have a house office." He's taking over Rowena's room as well as mine, paying two-thirds of the rent here so nothing will change for Hunter. "And of course living with a woman will be better than having to deal with your pre-dawn blender smoothie rituals." He winks at Hunter.

And my friend promptly chokes on her tea, flushing scarlet. Oh yeah, she definitely has it bad for my brother. Poor thing. How did I never notice? Maybe the fact that they're going to live together has put her on edge, and she's less able to hide it.

I glance at Rowena, who is staring listlessly into her mug, complexion ashen. A lump lodges in my throat. I wish I could do more for her. Just then, her phone buzzes. She checks the screen and sighs.

"It's him," she says flatly. "Asking if I need help with the move. He offered to send 'his people' over."

"Ooh, 'his people,'" Dylan echoes with exaggerated awe. "Exactly how loaded is this guy, huh?"

"Very," Rowena replies, tight-lipped.

I scoot closer and put an arm around her thin shoulders. "Hey, at least he's nice. He's offering to help."

"He'd be nicer if he offered to help in person," Hunter tuts.

I stare daggers at her, can't she see Rowena is barely keeping it together?

"He must be busy." Turning again to my pregnant friend, I add, "You know we're here for you, right? No matter what you decide. Marriage, baby, all of it—if you change your mind at any point, we'll support you."

Rowena's eyes fill with tears. She sets down her mug and hugs me fiercely.

I stroke her silky hair, wishing I could take some of her pain away and help her carry it.

I try to lighten the mood with a joke. "Hey, and if the guy is so loaded, you should tell him to have 'his people' over and pack my stuff too."

Rowena's chest starts shaking with laughter instead of sobs. "I'm sorry," she says, pulling back. "Pregnancy hormones have turned me into a mess. I'll be fine, really. The guy works so much I'll barely see him, and there are worse destinies than having a penthouse all to myself."

At least she hasn't lost her sense of humor.

We finish our teas and return to packing, with a different energy. A new vibe. I glance over at Hunter meticulously dividing our mugs collection, Rowena carefully boxing her books, and Dylan hefting stacks of boxes marked "Kitchen." Beneath the bustle of activity, there's an unspoken current of love and support binding us together.

"I never thought I'd say this, but I might actually miss your snoring, Hunt," I tease her, taping up a box of bedding.

She tosses a balled-up piece of wrapping paper at me. "Hey, I do *not* snore!"

"I heard that!" Dylan calls from the hall. "Should I buy earplugs before moving in?"

Hunter stares daggers at me. "I don't snore," she hisses again.

I bump her hip with mine. "I'm sure Dylan won't mind."

"What's that supposed to mean?"

I give her a teasing grin. "Nothing."

As I drop yet another box by the door, I catch Rowena as she sighs over a framed photo of her and Liam, her ex, the father of the baby. Choosing to leave a toxic relationship is never easy, but she's showing such courage and strength. I'm in awe of her. I just hope that by marrying a rando she isn't rolling out of the frying pan into the fire.

But even if she does, we'll be here to catch her—*them*, her baby is already part of the family. I stare at the people beside me who, apart from Dylan, who I'm actually related to, are like a second family. And bask in the certainty that no matter where life brings us, we'll always be there for each other.

Later, Tristan and I are alone in my room, packing the last few items. He picks up the snow globe from my nightstand, the one with the selfie we took in New Haven last Christmas. I feel a rush of affection at the memory.

"Remember when I had to sneak this into your room at the crack of dawn?" he muses, shaking the globe.

"Mmm, it feels like a lifetime ago," I agree, moving to slip my arms around him from behind. "All the hiding and sneaking around."

He sets the snow globe in a box and turns to face me, hands settling on my hips. "No more of that. From now on, it's you and me against the world. Think you can handle having me around twenty-four-seven?"

I loop my arms behind his neck. "My dear prince, I've been handling you for months. It's you who might not survive me," I quip, poking his chest with a finger. I lower my hand over his heart, fisting the soft fabric of his T-shirt and pulling him toward me. "I'm very high maintenance, in case you hadn't noticed."

He beams, eyes crinkling. "Oh, I know just how high maintenance you can be. But trust me"—he flicks my nose before his arm circles my waist—"you're not nearly as high maintenance when you love me as when you hate me."

He kisses me then, tender and full of unspoken promises. I melt into him, awash in giddy anticipation to wake next to him every morning.

Once we break apart and Tristan disappears down the hall with the last of my boxes, I take one last look around the empty room—once my safe haven, now a blank canvas for someone else's story. The girl who moved in here, guarded and unsure about her looks, is not the same woman who's leaving. With a deep breath, I close the door on who I was and step forward into who I'm meant to become.

ACKNOWLEDGMENTS

If you're reading this, it means you've either finished the book or skipped to the end (no judgment here). Thank you for coming on this wild, romantic ride. I hope it left you more in love with love, and maybe, just a little bit more in love with reading.

As for my other expression of gratitude. First, a shoutout to coffee, the true unsung hero of this journey, and to my laptop, who, despite all odds, didn't crash. You both deserve a vacation.

Massive thanks to my editor, Megan Haslam, for making sure Tristan became his best book boyfriend self. To my copy editor, Cecily Blench, for checking the fine print. And to my proofreader, Candida Bradford, for helping me smooth out those last few imperfections—if only anti-cellulite lotion worked as wonderfully as she does.

To the production team at Boldwood Books for wrapping my story in tinsel and pretty formatting. To the marketing and sales teams who work relentlessly to make my stories reach more readers like you. And to everyone else at Boldwood who works behind the scenes.

A gigantic thank you to the world's best support crew. To my partner, who has mastered the art of the supportive nod and the strategic coffee delivery. Your belief in my "just one more revision" at 2 a.m. has not gone unnoticed. To my family, who endured endless "Do you want to hear a funny scene I just wrote?" moments at dinner and still asked for seconds. I owe you all big time.

To the book-loving community, bloggers and influencers, for helping to share the book love.

And lastly, to you, dear reader. Thank you for laughing and crying in all the right places (and even in some unexpected ones). If my characters have found a little home in your heart, then every sleep-deprived night was worth it. Here's to more adventures together, with love and laughter leading the way!

ABOUT THE AUTHOR

Camilla Isley is an engineer who left science behind to write bestselling contemporary rom-coms set all around the world. She lives in Italy.

Sign up to Camilla Isley's mailing list for news, competitions and updates on future books.

Visit Camilla's website: https://camillaisley.com/

Follow Camilla on social media here:

facebook.com/camillaisley

x.com/camillaisley

instagram.com/camillaisley

bookbub.com/authors/camilla-isley

ALSO BY CAMILLA ISLEY

The Love Theorem

Love Quest

The Love Proposal

Love To Hate You

Not In A Billion Years

Baby, One More Time

It's Complicated

The Love Algorithm

It Started With A Book

The Is Not a Holiday Romance

WHERE ALL YOUR ROMANCE DREAMS COME TRUE!

THE HOME OF BESTSELLING ROMANCE AND WOMEN'S FICTION

 WARNING:
MAY CONTAIN SPICE

SIGN UP TO OUR
NEWSLETTER

https://bit.ly/Lovenotesnews

Boldwood

Boldwood Books is an award-winning fiction publishing company seeking out the best stories from around the world.

Find out more at www.boldwoodbooks.com

Join our reader community for brilliant books, competitions and offers!

Follow us

@BoldwoodBooks

@TheBoldBookClub

Sign up to our weekly deals newsletter

https://bit.ly/BoldwoodBNewsletter

Made in United States
Troutdale, OR
12/14/2024

26468755R00126